CURIOUSER AND...

JILLIAN MARIA

Trigger Warnings:

On-page depiction of a panic attack/flashback, on-page depiction of dissociation, detailed (verbal) description of depression, ableism toward mental health issues — including internalized ableism (this is refuted on-page), discussion of a suicide (does not give specifics of the method, only the emotions that led up to it), discussions of grief/mortality/similar topics, somewhat graphic (verbal) description of a physical illness, somewhat graphic body horror, brief mentions of homophobia (nothing violent), character death.

Prologue

The tale of Ashlyn Jones is a peculiar one.

It certainly isn't appropriate for the children who flock to my library, sitting in a large circle on the carpet for story time. I read them tales with simple lessons and happy, uncomplicated endings—tales where the heroes always get exactly what they want and the villains always get exactly what they deserve. Ashlyn's story is none of these things.

I would tell it to adults, if they'd only ask. But they wouldn't, even if they knew to do so. When adults come to my library, they come with their adult egos and adult minds, with their adult beliefs and adult impatience. Why would they sit and listen to an old man recite a whimsical tale that cuts into their precious time?

So, too often, Ashlyn's story goes untold. But not always.

They come to me when story time ends—sometimes alone, but more often in pairs. They're old enough to have outgrown the circle on the carpet, but they're not yet old enough to have unlearned the act of listening.

Those children-who-are-not-quite-children find me. And they ask me for a story.

When that happens, I lead them through the shelves, to the quietest part of the library. I settle them into the large armchairs next to the window. The library's resident cat will usually find its way over, making a purring home on one of their laps.

And, when they're ready and listening, I begin.

Through The Well

Ashlyn Jones was an obedient child (although, at sixteen, she might have privately balked at anyone referring to her as a "child"). She did not sneak out past curfew or curse at her parents. She didn't drink herself into a stupor or come home with the smell of smoke clinging to her sweater. She didn't even sneak into R-rated movies. She was not, in short, the sort of child written of in these cautionary tales.

This was not enough to save her.

It happened on a day in November, too early for snow but late enough in the year that the trees were brittle and bare, the wind taking on a sharp, glassy quality. It was, in truth, too cold for many people to be in the cabins gathered among the trees, but Ashlyn's parents wanted to visit a nearby aunt, and so they had gone.

Ashlyn stared out the window as they drove through the woods. The chill emanating even from the closed window was a bit uncomfortable, and they'd missed the leaves at their most vibrant, leaving only brown soil underfoot and bare, skinny branches. She opened her mouth to say it was a shame they hadn't come a few weeks earlier, then closed it. Even if she meant it as a neutral topic of conversation, her mother would interpret it as a complaint, and she hated it when Ashlyn complained.

Instead of commenting on the weather, Ashlyn glanced backward. "I saw a roller rink back in town. Do you think you could drive me to it later?"

"You don't want to go to a place like that," her father replied. "Some grimy dump with a bunch of delinquents loitering outside? No daughter of mine would be caught hanging around those types."

Ashlyn knew the group he was talking about. She wondered, a little, what made her father write them off—maybe it was the fact that their clothes all seemed worn out, or maybe it was the very conspicuous rainbow patch that one of the girls wore on the arm of her jean jacket. But they had seemed warm, and friendly, and something about the girl's smile had made her feel safe.

It probably wasn't fair for her father to judge them so harshly. Perhaps a different person would try to defend them. But what was the point? It wasn't as though Ashlyn would change his mind. Instead, she merely said, "Okay, Papa," and returned to staring out the window.

They made their way to the cabin. The moment she was alone in her own room, Ashlyn pressed her back up against the door, squeezing her eyes shut. The words she had swallowed—about the weather, about the roller rink, about a thousand other inconsequential things—welled up in her throat, threatening to choke her.

She wrapped her arms about her shoulders, forcing breath into her tight lungs. "Stop that," she scolded herself in a whisper. She was being dramatic. Why was she so often like this? She was lucky she had managed to hold it all in until she was alone. There was no need to bother her parents while they were on vacation with one of her silly *moods*.

She needed to look on the bright side—perhaps literally. The sun was unseasonably bright, after all, dulling the edges of the season's chill.

Resolving to take advantage of it, she made her way down the hall. "Mama," she said to her mother, who sat knitting in the living room. "May I go out into the forest and read?"

Her mother looked up from her project, humming. "That's fine," she said. "But be sure to take a heavier sweater, or you'll catch a chill. Why don't you wear that lovely pale blue one that matches your eyes? And while you're at it, the white pants will match it so much nicer than the ones you have on."

Were such light colors really appropriate for walking through the forest? Ashlyn had her doubts, but she would no sooner argue with her mother over clothes than she would with her father over the roller rink. Besides, it was better to bring a blanket than sit in the dirt, anyway. "Okay," she said, and changed.

"There's my girl," her mother said when she returned. "Here, one moment. You've got your hair in your eyes again."

Ashlyn didn't think the side-swept bangs were that long, but her mother had a strange fixation with them. She stayed still as her mother fussed over her, tying a black ribbon in her straight, sandy blonde hair, using it to hold back her bangs like a headband while keeping the rest to fall down her back.

Apparently satisfied, her mother smiled, pinching her cheeks in a way that only a mother would. "My dear little doll," she said. "Be home for dinner, will you?"

"Of course, Mama," Ashlyn said. It was a promise she had every intention of keeping.

Ashlyn ventured into the forest with her

blanket and her book. Even this late in the year, the forest had plenty of charms. It smelled of dirt and dead leaves, yes, but also pine and some ineffable scent that Ashlyn could only assume was the smell of life.

She found a clearing to spread out her blanket in, and settled down to read. The sound of wind through the tree branches made a pleasant enough backdrop for her reading, and she got through several chapters of her book in cheerful solitude.

But eventually, another sound began to encroach upon her afternoon. It was high-pitched, rough and organic and a little too *aware* to be from the non-sentient trees. It sounded, in fact, an awful lot like the cries of an animal in distress. Ashlyn frowned, pausing in her reading. The cries grew louder, more anguished, and she couldn't bear to leave it to suffer its fate all alone.

Still, Ashlyn was not a fool, so it was carefully that she crept in the direction of the noise. If the animal was in danger, she would have to take care not to allow that same danger to befall her, whatever it was—a predator like a bear or a wolf, perhaps, or a trap that she could injure herself trying to pry open.

But when she finally found the source of the noise, it seemed to be neither of those things. A rabbit seemed trapped, in fact, but not by sharp metal or rough rope. Instead, it struggled against old, gnarled branches spread across the ground. It screamed out into the forest, such a big noise coming from such a small creature.

"You poor thing!" exclaimed Ashlyn, moving forward. "Please don't cry. I'll help you."

Moving carefully to avoid bites, Ashlyn set to work, adjusting the branches until they had loosened enough to free the rabbit from its fate. The rabbit, not knowing enough to thank its rescuer, disappeared with a mad dash into the forest, vanishing into the trees with only a flick of white tail. Ashlyn smiled, watching it go.

"Be more careful next time, little friend," she said sweetly—and somewhat ironically, for of course she knew that the rabbit did not understand her words.

Curlous, she examined the place that had trapped the creature so. It was a stranger sight than she anticipated: the rabbit's foot seemed to have punched straight through the earth, a circle of endless black beyond the top layer of branches and leaves. But that didn't make sense—how could such short legs have created a hole so deep that Ashlyn couldn't see the bottom? It was almost as if she were kneeling over a chasm, a black pit covered by only the thinnest layer of earth.

If Ashlyn hadn't been so distracted, she might have noticed that the ground felt a bit strange as she walked on it. If the rabbit hadn't been screaming, perhaps she would have heard the hollow sound her footsteps made. But she had, and it had, and so Ashlyn had no way of realizing that she now knelt over an old well, boarded up by wood that was beginning to rot.

A groan sounded beneath her as the wood, unaccustomed to the weight of a whole person pressing against it, finally collapsed in on itself. Much like the rabbit, Ashlyn cried out, but unlike the rabbit, there was no one there to hear her. And so, alone, Ashlyn Jones tumbled into the dark.

Through The Trees

shlyn opened her eyes to a dark sky.

It was dusk, at that time where it was only just too light for stars. As she stared up at the gray-blue expanse, Ashlyn gasped, worry plucking at her veins. She had promised her mother that she would be home for dinner. She'd be scolded for being late.

But, as memories returned to her, she realized she had more to worry about than just missing dinner. She had fallen down a well, she remembered, but stone and dirt didn't surround her. Trees did, and not the bare trees she'd been sitting among when she read. No, although it seemed even colder now than it had earlier, these trees still had leaves on them—half-dead but clinging stubbornly to life on the gray branches.

Ashlyn ordinarily loved the sight of changing leaves. But these were all wrong, and not just because it wasn't the season for them. The browns and oranges and yellows were too muted, too strange, and there were no red leaves at all. "*What* is going on?" she asked.

One thing was clear: she was no longer in a forest she knew. The trees were taller than any trees Ashlyn had ever seen, their branches twisting up into the sky like claws. She laid on a dirt path, the earth beneath her cold and smelling faintly of metal. Ahead of her, there was a wooden sign attached to a fence post.

Ashlyn stood carefully, wary of injuries. Her legs bore her weight well enough, however, and she didn't *feel* injured. A little confused, and more than a little frightened, and even more than a little cold, but not injured. The worst damage seemed to be her clothes, which were now torn and covered in dirt. The ribbon her mother tied in her hair was nowhere to be found, and she was missing one of her black, flat-soled shoes. Wincing as she imagined her mother's reprimand, she made her way to the sign, hoping for some guidance.

THIS WAY, it read in bold black lettering. Ashlyn frowned. What was "this" supposed to mean? Even if she'd known the answer to that question, it wouldn't have made any difference—the sign bore no arrow, no marker, no indication of what direction it meant to lead her.

Was this some sort of joke?

No sooner had the thought crossed her mind than a black shape appeared, blurring out of trees as if by magic. Ashlyn let out a cry, startling backward. But it was only a cat, coming to balance on the top of the sign. A more superstitious person might have found the cat's black fur unnerving, but Ashlyn was not superstitious, and so she only laughed softly.

"You startled me, little friend," she said.

The cat regarded her with a yellow gaze. Then, it smiled at her with a set of perfectly even human teeth.

"*Oh*," Ashlyn said, then fell silent. It seemed to her that she should have had more to say on this development, but presently nothing occurred to her. She could only stare, and wonder just a little if she had hit her head too hard in the fall. Maybe all of this was some strange hallucination. Perhaps a dream.

The cat licked its paw, looking for all the world like a normal feline. It stretched, still balanced on top of that perplexing sign, and then it leapt with quiet grace to the forest floor. It trotted in that way cats had, seeming to have a purpose known only to itself.

"Where are you going?" Ashlyn asked, a fair bit less ironically than when she had addressed the rabbit earlier. This was far from a normal cat. It seemed to know things. And for Ashlyn, who felt as though she knew less with every passing second, following the cat seemed almost logical.

The cat led her on a winding chase. It never once left the dirt path to vanish among the trees, and the more she walked, the more Ashlyn became convinced that the cat meant for her to follow it. It seemed to slow to allow her to keep up and even glanced over its shoulder a time or two.

"What do you *want*?" Ashlyn had enough presence of mind to feel a bit sheepish, for as strange as the cat seemed, it hadn't spoken yet. She had no reason to believe it would start now.

They arrived at a fork in the road. The cat planted itself right in the center, turning around to regard Ashlyn with its yellow gaze as if to ask what she thought. Even if Ashlyn could find her voice to speak, she would not have known what to say.

At the fork in the road, there was a tree. And a girl. Only it was hard to tell where one ended and the other began.

The girl seemed to be around sixteen as well, and Ashlyn thought she was rather beautiful, although it was hard to tell in her present condition. Her torso was all caught up in the tree's great gray trunk, bark growing over her stomach and chest and legs, catching on her simple white dress. Her outstretched arms twined with the branches, fingertips upturned toward the sky. Strands of her long, wavy brown hair caught on the bark. Her eyes were closed and her skin was not just pale but faintly *blue*, as though Ashlyn were looking at a corpse.

But the girl was not dead. Ashlyn could see her breath, transient clouds of pale white on the cold air.

"What is this?" Ashlyn murmured to herself, before raising her voice to address the girl. "Hello?" The girl did not stir. Ashlyn shifted her weight from foot to foot. "Can you hear me?"

Still, there was no response. The cat, who had been eyeing her carefully, gave another great stretch before sauntering off into the trees. Ashlyn looked at it and then back to the girl. Which was more practical to focus her attention on at the moment? In the time it took her to decide, the cat vanished.

"Oh, dear," murmured Ashlyn. She regretted not following the cat when she had the chance—as strange as it had been, it was the closest thing she had to a guide.

She looked around, hoping for some clue of where to go next. But there was no sign, no indication of where either path might lead. There was only the girl in the tree, and she didn't seem inclined to answer.

With no other options, Ashlyn approached

her. Up close, she could see the shallow rise and fall of the girl's chest, the way her breath stirred the loose strands of brown hair that fell over her forehead. For a moment, Ashlyn felt a very awkward urge to push that hair away from her face, but of course that was an awful intimate gesture to give any stranger, much less a sleeping one, and so she refrained.

Before she could think of her next move, however, a growl cut through the forest.

Ashlyn gasped, jerking away from the sleeping girl. She turned to see a frightening sight indeed: several wolves stalked down one path toward her, their snouts low to the ground. Now, Ashlyn was no expert in wolves, but even she could see that these were not ordinary ones. Their shoulders were too broad and hulking, their snouts too long. Their teeth were razor sharp and dripping with saliva. They looked more like a child's nightmare than real animals.

While frightening, this did, in its way, solve the mystery of which direction to take. Ashlyn put her back to the wolves, and she ran.

The wolves gave chase after her. She could hear the thundering of their paws, the snarling of their breath. Ashlyn forced her feet to move faster, even as her chest began to ache and her breath began to thicken in her lungs. She wasn't sure where she was running to, but she knew what she was running from, and that seemed altogether more pressing at that moment. She turned the corner, hoping for something, anything.

What she found was the girl, still sleeping in her tree.

The path had not seemed to double in on itself. But this was the same tree, the same girl, the same fork in the road. Too shocked to pay attention to her steps, Ashlyn stumbled over her own feet, falling hard at the base of the tree. The wolves were at her back.

"Help!" Ashlyn shouted as the wolves closed in. "Someone, please!"

Ashlyn ducked, cowering with her hands held over the back of her neck. But the sickening impact of fur and teeth and pain never came. Instead, there was a strange crunching noise. The wolves howled. But they did not descend on her.

Ashlyn turned. Each and every wolf was trapped, pinned in place by sharp tree branches. Blood frothed in the corners of their snarling mouths, but none of it belonged to Ashlyn. It belonged to them.

Ashlyn faced the tree once again. Only it wasn't a tree, not anymore—it had been rent into pieces. The girl floated in mid-air among the wreckage, her wavy brown hair moving as if underwater. Her eyes were open, but they were pure white and glowing, and her face was as slack as any other dreamer's.

She hung there for several seconds more,

suspended as if on string. Long enough for the wolves to grow quiet as they succumbed to their wounds. Only then did the light vanish from her eyes, and she dropped.

Ashlyn reached out quite without thinking, catching her. The weight sent her tumbling to the ground, a clumsy affair that only further covered the both of them in dirt. Not that the girl seemed to mind overmuch. She was sleeping again.

"What *is* this?" Ashlyn asked. "Can you hear me?"

A rustling echoed through the forest, and Ashlyn clutched the sleeping girl closer on instinct. A man stepped out of the trees. He was tall and gangling, with tan skin and dark hair in loose curls about his face. A black ribbon encircled his throat, and a matching top hat sat on his head. He placed his hands on his hips, looking from the dead wolves to Ashlyn and the unconscious girl in her arms. Then, he smiled.

"Well, well," he said. "Curiouser a—"

Another figure burst out of the forest.

This was also a man, but he was shorter and rounder than the man with the top hat. He had black hair shot through with gray and golden skin lined with wrinkles. "Oh, no. What is this mess?" He pulled up the sleeve of his crisp white button-down, examining his gold wristwatch. "Oh, this is going to take ages to clean up, and we simply don't have the time!"

"Oh, dear." A woman with a black afro stepped out behind him, picking her way over the wolf corpses in vintage platform boots. She was muscular, her dark skin littered with scars, but her eyes were kind as she looked at Ashlyn. "It seems as though you two have had quite the fight. Are you alright?"

Horrifyingly, Ashlyn found herself near tears. "I don't *know*," she said. "I don't know what's happening, I don't know where I am, I don't know who this girl is. I don't know anything."

The man with the top hat clicked his tongue. "You must be a newcomer!" He gave a flourishing bow. "Let me be the first to introduce you. And guide you, if you wish. This forest is many things, but it isn't a place to be wandering alone."

"What?" The shorter man nearly exploded. "We don't have time to help some girl!"

"Why? Do you have more pressing matters to attend to?"

"Of course not! Who has the time for that?"

"Ignore them," the woman said, her voice kind. "Merrick is right, though. You should come with us. It's not safe here."

Of course, Ashlyn knew better than to follow strangers anywhere in ordinary circumstances. But these were far from ordinary circumstances, and Ashlyn was too frightened to put up a proper fight.

"Okay," she said.

- 4 -

Through The Round Door

The woman—Lucy, she introduced herself—carried the sleeping girl in her arms. Merrick, the man in the top hat, led the way as Kazuo, the older man, followed behind, muttering about the time.

Ashlyn wasn't sure what to make of them, any more than she knew what to make of this place. They seemed like an odd group, as though they had each come from wildly different functions. Kazuo wore a white button-down shirt and black pants that looked like they'd be at home in some corporate office; Lucy looked as though she had stepped out of some retro-themed party in her patterned blouse and flared jeans. And Merrick . . . Ashlyn couldn't even begin to guess at where Merrick came from, his top hat incongruous with his casual t-shirt and red pants.

And, yet, they seemed to all be part of the same group. Ashlyn didn't know how to ask about it—or perhaps she had too many pressing questions to decide what to ask first—and so they walked in silence through the wood.

The strange-colored trees seemed to stretch on forever—until they reached a cliffside. Ashlyn gasped at what she saw there. Below and in the distance, there were endless rows of vivid green hedges surrounding a shining castle. It seemed to be the brightest thing in this place. "What is that?" she asked.

Lucy's expression darkened. "That's the queen's castle," she said. "You don't want to be caught there. It's the most dangerous place of all."

She said it with such conviction that Ashlyn had to suppress a shiver. The clearing ended, and the trees once again concealed the castle from view. A few moments later, they came upon a large circular door halfway sunk into the ground, as if leading to some underground tunnel. Only Merrick opened it to reveal a low-ceilinged home, one with chairs and tables and even a fireplace.

"Welcome!" he said.

Kazuo immediately darted into the kitchen, still muttering. Ashlyn followed Merrick and Lucy into a small bedroom, where Lucy laid the sleeping girl down. She looked altogether healthier than when she'd been tangled up in the tree, her skin no longer tinged blue. But she still didn't stir as Lucy fussed over her. Ashlyn hovered behind her for a moment, then sat down on a small chair next to the bed. Merrick sprawled in an armchair against the far wall, regarding her with dark eyes that seemed caught between blue and brown.

"So," he said. "What do you want to know?"

Ashlyn breathed out. "*Everything*."

Merrick raised an eyebrow. "That's quite the tall order, but I suppose we can go alphabetically. Let's start with aardvarks. They're a burrowing mammal native to Africa, and—"

"No!" Ashlyn interrupted. "I mean, everything about this. What is this place, and how did I get here?"

"This is my home, and we walked."

"Quit teasing the girl, Merrick," Lucy scolded. She turned to Ashlyn, cocking her head to the side. "What's your name, dear? And how did you get here?"

"I'm Ashlyn," she said. "I . . . I fell down an old well in the forest. Then I was here."

"I see." Lucy hummed out a quiet, sympathetic noise. "I'm so sorry. That sounds very frightening."

"Wait, how did *you* get here?"

Lucy's expression turned strange, and

Merrick tapped a finger to his chin. "You know, I'm not sure I can quite recall. The last thing I remember, I was driving to rehearsal." He smiled at Ashlyn, as though they were both in on some joke. "Clearly, I took a wrong turn."

"But that doesn't make any sense!" Ashlyn cried. "How could you get here on a wrong turn, if I got here on a fall?"

Merrick shrugged. "How does the sun rise every morning and set every evening? How do cats always land on their feet? How do people care for each other in spite of everything? Some things simply *are*, my dear, and are better left unquestioned."

This struck Ashlyn as a rather imperfect comparison, but she decided against arguing it. She turned to Lucy instead. "What about you? Can you make sense of any of this?"

It took several seconds for Lucy to respond. Ashlyn got the impression that she was trying to find the right words to express herself, rather than being unsure of the answer itself. "Sense . . . is difficult to come by here. I'm sure you've noticed that this isn't like any place you've ever seen. The sky never brightens or darkens—it's always dusk. The animals are strange and unfamiliar. And the paths loop in on each other in impossible, nonsensical directions. Along the way, it's easy for things to get . . . lost."

"And found," Merrick added in a near singsong. "And lost again. Best not to dwell on it too wretchedly, or the thing you lose next may be your head." He tipped his hat in Ashlyn's direction with a wink.

Ashlyn shivered, wrapping her arms around herself. "Well, how do I get home?"

Lucy and Merrick exchanged a look. It was a look that Ashlyn—and, indeed, all children—knew well: a look between adults about to break very bad news to someone much younger than them. Ashlyn's heart sank, and she knew the answer long before Lucy spoke.

"There *is* no way to leave here. I'm so sorry."

Pressure built up in the back of Ashlyn's throat, and she wasn't sure if she meant to scream or cry or—or lose her head, as Merrick put it. In the back of her mind, she heard her mother chide her, reminding her not to be so dramatic. Carefully, she pulled in a breath, then let it out. Her frantic gaze landed on the sleeping girl, still lying still on the bed.

"What about her?" she blurted.

If Lucy thought the change in topic strange, she didn't question it. "I'm not sure. She's been sleeping in that tree longer than any of us have been here. We tried to get her out, but nothing worked."

"Nothing but you," Merrick said. "You must be a special girl indeed."

Ashlyn thought about this for a long

moment, staring at the sleeping girl's face in silence. "If I'm so special," she murmured. "I should be able to find a way out of here."

"Ashlyn . . ." Lucy started.

"No." Ashlyn looked up, her blue eyes hard and her young face very, very determined. "No, I refuse to believe I am trapped here. I'm going to find a way home. I'm going to find a way back to my parents. Everything is going to go back to normal. Everything is going to be fine."

Lucy opened her mouth as if to argue, but a look from Merrick silenced her. "You've just had a shock," she said kindly. "We'll give you some time to absorb all of this." With one last check on the sleeping girl, she walked from the room. Merrick remained only long enough to give Ashlyn a wink, as though to suggest that he, at least, believed in her claim.

As the door clicked behind him, the resolve drained from Ashlyn's body like water. She slipped to her knees by the bed, curling her fists in the blankets like a small, frightened child.

"Please, wake up," said Ashlyn, her voice very small. "If you've been here longer than anyone, you must know *something* that will help me get home. And you protected me, I think, back there with the wolves. Please, I'm very frightened, and I need your help again."

In spite of her spoken reasons, Ashlyn wasn't *really* sure why she wanted the sleeping girl awake. It just seemed very important, suddenly, important in a way she couldn't begin to understand or explain.

She looked up. The girl's eyes were open, not glowing but a deep, forest green.

"Oh!" Ashlyn said. "You're awake."

"I'm awake," the girl echoed, her voice low and raspy with sleep. She touched her throat, puzzled. "I'm awake?" Her green gaze locked with Ashlyn's blue one. "You . . . You asked for help. I answered, because you asked for help. Why?"

Was this girl questioning Ashlyn, or herself? Ashlyn only had the answer to one of those questions, so that was what she offered. "I'm trying to find a way out of this forest. And it sounds like you've been here longer than anyone that I've talked to, so I hoped that maybe . . . maybe you could help me?"

"You hoped. Hope." The girl spoke the word with an odd inflection, like someone trying out a foreign language for the first time. Her gaze went far away for a moment, but then sharpened. "What's your name?"

"Oh! Sorry. I'm Ashlyn." Heat rushed to Ashlyn's cheeks. In all of this, she had quite forgotten her manners. "What's your name?"

"Azalea." The girl's gaze had gone distant again. "I am Azalea. You are Ashlyn. And you are . . . hopeful."

"Excuse me," Ashlyn said quietly. "But *can* you help me?"

Azalea brought her gaze to Ashlyn's once more, looking as though it took a significant amount of effort for her to do so. She looked tired. There were slight bags under her eyes, as though she'd been sleeping far less than Lucy's claim. "I'm sorry," she said. "I can't give you the answers you're looking for."

"Oh." A weight settled on Ashlyn's chest. She looked down, blinking against the stinging in her eyes. She didn't want to be dramatic by bursting into tears. "Well, I—"

"I can't give you answers, but if you mean to look for a way out, I'll join you."

"What?" Ashlyn looked up, eyes wide. "You'd do that? Why?"

Azalea frowned. "I don't know." She sounded as surprised as Ashlyn felt. "But I will. If you'd like me to, I mean."

Ashlyn took a deep breath. This place still seemed overwhelming and frightening. But, somehow, the idea of facing it with Azalea by her side made her feel just a bit more hopeful. It defied sense, since this was a girl she did not truly know. But in a situation like this, Ashlyn decided it was wise to take her comfort where she could get it.

"I would," she said. "Thank you."

-5-

Through The Wardrobe

"**I**f you're going to go walking through the forest, you'll both need a change of clothes."

Ashlyn looked down at her torn blue sweater, her filthy white pants, her missing shoe. She wouldn't last far in that condition. And Azalea, now standing beside her, seemed ill-equipped for the chill in her white dress.

"You have a point," she conceded. "Do you have anything for us to wear?"

"Of course!" Merrick replied. "No self-respecting actor would go without proper costumes. I'm sure you'll find something that suits you."

With a flourish, Merrick threw open a door to reveal the biggest and strangest walk-in closet

Ashlyn had ever seen. Archaic cloaks and old-fashioned dresses sat side-by-side with modern jeans and t-shirts, with every decade in-between present and accounted for. Accessories ranged from the practical—belts and sunglasses—to the truly impractical—feather boas and hats that shed glitter everywhere. Was *this* why everyone in the group dressed so radically different from one another?

Azalea walked inside, looking around. "These all seem to be my size," she mused.

"Well, of course," Merrick said. "You're the one trying to find an outfit."

Azalea nodded as if this made sense, picking out clothing with ease: a beige sweater with a brown wool dress to go overtop it, a brown belt and sturdy boots with a pair of thick, warm stockings to wear underneath. Once she finished, she looked over at Ashlyn, who still hovered in the doorway. "Are you alright?"

"I'm fine," Ashlyn said. "It's just . . . goodness, there's so much clothing here to choose from."

Azalea paused for a moment, then nodded. "You're overwhelmed. That's understandable. What do you like to wear, generally?"

Ashlyn thought about this for a long moment. "I'm not sure," she said. "My mother usually picks out my clothes for me."

"You have *no* preferences?"

Ashlyn wasn't sure how to answer that. Not

because she didn't have preferences, but because she wasn't sure why that mattered. There seemed to be a thousand rules about what was appropriate to wear in any given circumstance, and Ashlyn couldn't trust her own judgment. She wouldn't even know where to start.

"Could you pick something out for me?" she asked.

Azalea stared for a long moment. The silence between them felt loaded, reminding Ashlyn of waiting for the doctor to arrive before a check-up, sitting in a thin paper gown and trying not to shiver. She crossed her arms over her chest as Azalea picked up a blue sweater, then a black one.

"Which of these do you like better?" asked Azalea.

"What?"

"Speak quickly."

"I don't *know*." That uncomfortable sense of vulnerability only grew. "The black one?"

"Good." Azalea put aside the blue sweater, and picked up a purple sweater to hold up beside the black one instead. "What about between these two?"

"You can't be serious," said Ashlyn, who by now was catching on to Azalea's plan. "Can't you pick out something for me?"

"Pick something for you . . ." Azalea frowned, her gaze drifting over Ashlyn's shoulder. "It would be less overwhelming . . . but it would also make you less *yourself.* There's danger in that, too, you know. You exist but you don't live. It starts so slow. In little things. Decisions you can't bring yourself to make. But then . . ." She trailed off.

"Azalea?" Ashlyn called hesitantly.

Azalea blinked, gaze focusing on Ashlyn once again. "I'm sorry. I'm still a bit . . . scattered. Confusing waking moments with old dreams. Ignore me." She held up the sweaters again. "You should pick your own clothes. I'll help, but the final decision needs to be yours. It's a small thing in your control, but even a small thing is better than nothing, don't you agree?"

Ashlyn had no reply to this. For as long as she'd been alive, there was very little that she decided on without at least one of her parents' approval. It was simply the way things were. But as Azalea stared at her, she found herself unable—or perhaps unwilling—to disagree.

"I like the purple one better," she said in a tone of acceptance.

Together like that, they were able to piece together an outfit: first a dark blue hooded sweater, then jeans, followed by a pair of sneakers, a beanie and gray fingerless gloves. Her mother would probably call those gloves impractical, but her mother was not here, and Ashlyn liked them. Maybe that was enough.

Merrick led Ashlyn to a small washroom, where she was able to clean up and get changed. When she looked at herself in the mirror, she found that she looked quite different from usual. Yet, she did not feel as though she didn't recognize herself. On the contrary, she felt as though she were *seeing* herself for the first time.

In other circumstances, this might have warranted some quiet time for introspection. These were not other circumstances, however, and Ashlyn very much wanted to get home. She opened the door.

Azalea was already dressed, her wavy brown hair now contained to a single braid that fell down her back. She looked at Ashlyn as she walked into the room, her green eyes calm and nearly grave. "You're ready," she said, more statement than question.

"I am." Ashlyn clasped her hands at her waist. "What do you think? Do you think the outfit is okay?"

"Do *you* like it?"

Had she been anyone else, Ashlyn might have worried that this was Azalea's way of dodging the question to be polite. But the question felt like a natural extension of their exercise in picking out an outfit. Ashlyn swallowed. "I do."

Azalea nodded. "Good. That matters far more than my opinion." After a pause, she added, "I *do* think it suits you, though."

Heat rose to Ashlyn's cheeks. "Thank you."

Merrick clapped, making Ashlyn jump—she'd hardly noticed him in the room. But he *was* in the room, gathered around a small table with Lucy and Kazuo. He winked, one elbow thrown over the back of his chair. "Well, then! Good luck on your adventure, young ones. I hope you find what you're looking for."

"Be careful," said Lucy. "Most of the forest is not dangerous, but it is easy to get lost. And do try to avoid the queen's castle."

"Which paths lead to the queen's castle?" asked Ashlyn.

"*All* paths lead to the queen's castle," Merrick replied.

This seemed rather ridiculous to Ashlyn, but at this point she decided better than to question it. "We will do our best, then."

"A waste of time," Kazuo muttered, surly. "Why do you want to waste time like that? Don't you know that we haven't got any?"

"What about this moment, right now?" Azalea asked. Her expression was calm, but there was an odd note in her voice. "Is this not time that we have?"

"Of course it isn't," Kazuo replied. "We have to find time before we have it, don't we? That only makes sense."

Azalea shrugged, seeming content enough to let the matter drop. Ashlyn cleared her throat. "Thank you," she said. "For everything."

There was a long moment of silence, then. A moment where Ashlyn thought that she ought to say something more. But nothing came to mind, and perhaps she was only delaying the inevitable. So, instead, she walked outside.

As Lucy had promised, it was still dusk. Ashlyn hesitated, staring into the trees. It seemed that the heroes of the stories she read always faced their challenges with endless courage and enthusiasm. But Ashlyn didn't feel particularly courageous or enthusiastic. Mostly, she just felt lost.

At least Azalea was by her side. *That* was something.

"What do you want to do?" Azalea asked.

Ashlyn took a deep breath. No matter how she felt, there was truly only one answer. "Let's start walking."

They did.

- 6 -

Through The Silent Wood

It took about five minutes of walking for Ashlyn's resolve to waver.

She wanted to return home. But how was she meant to do that? She longed for some kind of clue, the slightest hint that she was heading in the right direction. Even a sign as baffling as the one that had greeted her after her fall would have been welcome. But the dull autumn forest and the dull dusk sky stretched on, so uniform it was nearly dizzying.

And then, there was Azalea.

She hadn't said a word since they left Merrick's home. Her silence felt like a judgment, like a condemnation. Ashlyn could easily imagine her stewing, quietly ruminating on being dragged along on this pointless exercise.

Finally, she couldn't stand it. "I *know* it's bad, okay?"

Azalea blinked slowly. "What?"

There was no judgment in her tone, no anger or annoyance. Only a distant sort of confusion, like someone roused from a dream. Ashlyn's cheeks flushed. "I'm sorry," she said. "I thought I'd upset you. But I was jumping to conclusions." How often had her parents scolded her for letting her mind run ahead of her like that? In their absence, she scolded herself. "I'm being stupid."

"I wouldn't call that stupidity," Azalea replied. "Just . . . presumptuous. But I won't hold that against you. There are worse things to be." Was that a hint of humor in her voice?

Ashlyn cleared her throat. "So you aren't upset, then?"

"Why would I be?"

"Well," Ashlyn replied. "I don't have a plan. I don't have any clue what I'm doing. All I have is . . . is blind determination. It's not much."

Azalea was silent for a long moment. Then her face twisted, and she made a sharp noise that sounded a little like she had something stuck in her throat. She pressed a hand to her mouth, the corners of which were now turning up in a rather manic grin.

"Oh, I don't think I quite remember how to

laugh. Isn't that hideous?"

"Is what I said so funny?" Ashlyn asked, trying to ignore the part of her that was really rather put-out by the reaction.

"Not so funny, no," Azalea replied, although she was still smiling. "It's just . . . that sort of determination. I was thinking . . . well, that's more than *I* have. So maybe you should give yourself more credit."

Ashlyn found herself returning the smile. More ridiculously, she found herself battling giggles of her own. Perhaps this strange place was getting to her. "You aren't worried about wasting time? It seems like that's important to *some* people here."

"It is strange, isn't it?" Azalea shook her head. "To be so protective of time you can't do anything with. No, Ashlyn, I think my time with you is as well-spent as anything else. Plan or no plan."

"Oh." Ashlyn looked away, suddenly very interested in the tree line. "Well. I'm glad you're here, too. All of this would be much scarier if I was on my own."

Azalea was strange, it was true. Difficult to read, and distant in a dreamy sort of way. But when she focused on Ashlyn, it felt like she was *seeing* her. Ashlyn wasn't sure why that mattered, but it did.

She might have pondered that more, but at that moment they turned a corner on a strange sight, indeed. A grove of trees sat tucked along the side of the path, but instead of bearing fruits, they bore keys. They dangled from the branches, chiming gently in the breeze when they knocked into each other.

Ashlyn approached, giving one a tug. It appeared to be growing from the tree itself, not tied on by string. And no matter how hard she pulled, it wouldn't come off. "How very strange."

"Not so strange when you think about it," Azalea murmured. "There's not much use for keys in a place like this. Harvesting them wouldn't do much good."

"No, I mean . . . oh, I don't know *what* I mean." She shook her head, struck once again but just how strange their situation was. "What is this place, anyway?"

It was mostly a rhetorical question, so she startled a little when Azalea spoke. "The Lost One's Forest. The Silent Wood. The—Well. I won't belabor the point." She sighed, sounding tired again. "Different people have had different names for it. None stuck in a way that matters."

Ashlyn glanced over at her. "Did you hear those names before you fell asleep?"

Azalea's face twisted again, but this time there was no laugh, however disquieting, to accompany it. She didn't take her eyes off the keys. "Yes," she murmured.

There were questions Ashlyn wanted to ask,

then. How had Azalea ended up in that tree to begin with? How long had she been asleep? And what about Ashlyn made her wake up in the first place? But asking so bluntly felt too rude. It wasn't appropriate, to dig into the business of a relative stranger like that. So she stayed silent.

Finally, Azalea looked at her. Exhaustion clung to her green gaze, but it was still kind. "We should probably keep going," she said. "Unless you think the *key* to your escape is in this tree."

This time Ashlyn couldn't help it. She did laugh, tiny giggles spilling from between her fingers as she pressed them to her mouth. She even *snorted*, which her mother would have chided her for if she was around. "That was *terrible*."

"Perhaps I don't quite remember how to tell jokes, either," Azalea replied, smiling.

"Come *on*." They kept walking.

Only after a few turns, the forest opened up into a wide clearing, rolling hills made of strange brown grass. The castle stood on the other side, bright red walls and green hedges the most vibrant thing in this place even at a distance.

All roads led to the castle, Merrick had said. That, and the memory of Lucy's warning, sent a chill down Ashlyn's spine. And, yet, she couldn't bring herself to tear her eyes away. Dangerous or not, something compelled her.

"Maybe we shouldn't be avoiding it."

"What?"

Azalea's voice, unusually sharp, pulled Ashlyn from her thoughts. She blinked, turning to face her. "Just . . . If all roads end in the castle . . . what if the forest ends there, too? Maybe that's the way out. Don't you think it's at least possible?"

"No." Azalea grabbed Ashlyn by the wrists, her grip tight. "Ashlyn . . . you're not going to find the answers you want there. Believe me. Many have looked, and all . . . all of them . . ." She squeezed her eyes shut for a moment, then fixed Ashlyn in her most intense gaze yet. "You are hopeful. I am telling you, that is the place where hope goes to die."

Ashlyn didn't know what to do with this. With this sudden intensity, or with the sudden contact. Azalea's hands were warm.

"Okay," she finally said. "Okay. We'll . . . We'll stay away. I'm sure there's a way out of this forest somewhere else."

Azalea sighed, tension draining out of her body like water. "Good." She looked down at her own hands, as if surprised to see them gripping Ashlyn so intensely.

When she let go and stepped away, Ashlyn got the strangest sense that she was missing something.

7

Through The Mirrored Sky

Ashlyn couldn't get the castle out of her mind.

It wasn't so much that she didn't believe Azalea when she said that there wasn't anything for her there. But she rather doubted that she was getting the whole story. She almost broached the subject, several times, but she couldn't quite muster up the courage. Her parents often scolded her for being nosy, and Azalea was the closest thing she had to a friend in this place. Ashlyn didn't want to displease her.

Finally, she felt she had to ask *something*, even if it wasn't about the castle specifically. "Do you think there's anything we *should* aim for?"

Azalea blinked slowly, brow furrowing.

"What do you mean?"

"It's just . . . we're avoiding the castle, but we don't have anywhere to *go*." Ashlyn frowned at the dirt path in front of them. "You've been in this place a lot longer than I have. Isn't there anywhere worth looking into?"

"Worth. An interesting word." Azalea sighed, her own gaze drifting down the path much as Ashlyn's had done. "I'm not sure worth plays much of a role, though. Even if I could think of a place to go, I wouldn't know how to get there. The paths in this place are inconsistent. Following dream logic may be more beneficial than following a concrete plan." She glanced to Ashlyn then, smiling in a way that didn't quite reach her eyes. "Unfortunately, I'm no more expert in that than you are. My time spent sleeping was largely dreamless."

She said it like a joke, but Ashlyn couldn't much find the humor in their situation. "I guess we keep walking, then. I just wish something would happen."

"I wouldn't waste your energy on wishing," Azalea replied. "This place is full of somethings. You're bound to run into one, whether you want to or not."

As if to illustrate this slightly ominous statement, they turned a corner, and the path ended.

Although ended was perhaps the wrong word. A circle of mirror glass *interrupted* the path, spread out over the ground like a cold blanket. In its reflection, the dusk sky seemed off, its colors too dark. No trees grew on the glass, but around its edges they stood like sentinels, their reflections different in a way that Ashlyn couldn't quite process. The path picked up on the other side, maybe ten feet away.

Ashlyn held an arm out over the mirror, expecting to see her own pale hand reflected. But it wasn't. Just that endless expanse of dusk sky, unbroken even by stars. She shivered, withdrawing the hand to her chest.

The trees rustled, and on the other side of the mirror, a figure stepped onto the path.

At first, Ashlyn couldn't get much sense of the person—they wore a large black cloak that obscured the shape of their body, hood drawn low over their face—but their effect on Azalea was immediate. Her green eyes widened, her entire body stiffening as though turning to stone. But the figure didn't seem to notice either of them at all. They lowered their hood, revealing sharp, sallow features framed by long black hair with a widow's peak. Said features drew into an expression of panic far more palpable than the shock on Azalea's face.

"Not *another* one." They looked up, eyes wide—and noticed the two girls for the first time.

Azalea let out a quiet noise, audible only because the forest had gone so silent in that moment. For a second, the figure's expression slackened with shock, but they recovered quickly, drawing themself upright. "Azalea."

Ashlyn watched Azalea's chest rise and fall with the heave of one careful, measured breath. She still looked startled, but her voice came out even for all that. "Caul."

The figure—Caul, apparently—looked between Azalea and Ashlyn, a small frown on their lips. "You have a friend."

"She's not your concern," Azalea replied, her voice sharp. "Not *her* concern, either."

Ashlyn couldn't hold her tongue any longer. "Her? What are you talking about, how do you two know each other, what . . . what is going on?"

Caul sighed, pinching the bridge of their nose. "Those are all very involved questions, none of which I really want to get into. This" — and here they gestured at the circle of glass in front of them— "was supposed to be a patch of snake grass, but it's gone and moved on me, and now I'm going to have to track it down."

"Go, then." Ashlyn had never heard Azalea sound so cold. "Go and leave us alone."

But Caul didn't move. They looked to Ashlyn, their expression difficult to read. "What's your name?"

"*Don't* answer that," Azalea interjected before Ashlyn could speak. "That's not any of their business."

"Oh, Azalea." Caul shook their head slowly, and the strangest thing of all was that they almost sounded pitying. "If she wants your friend, she'll have her. Surely you know there's no use resisting her. The queen always gets her way in the end."

The queen. Ashlyn wasn't sure what unnerved her more: the mention of the sinister figure she'd heard so much about, or the tired resignation in Caul's voice.

Azalea looked to the forest floor. "Are you going to tell her I'm awake?"

"Do you really think she doesn't already know?" Caul sighed, shaking their head. That pity was back in their voice. "Why *did* you wake up, anyway?"

Azalea closed her eyes. "I don't know," she murmured.

"Ah. Well, that's a shame." Caul looked from her to Ashlyn, raising an eyebrow. "Do let me know if you find that snake grass, will you?" With that, they pulled their hood up and vanished into the trees.

For a long moment, all Ashlyn could think to do was stare after them. Then, she turned to Azalea. Her eyes were still closed, her arms wrapped around herself. She looked so *upset.* Perhaps if they had been closer, and had Ashlyn not felt so blindsided and confused in that moment, she might have offered a hug. At least some words of comfort.

But they *weren't* closer, and Ashlyn *did* feel confused and blindsided, so she stayed silent. Finally, Azalea looked up at her, green eyes wary. "Well?"

"Well, what?"

"You must have questions after all of that." Azalea gestured to the space that Caul had recently vacated.

Ashlyn looked down at the circle of glass. It continued to reflect nothing but that unnerving dim sky. "I've had questions for awhile now," she admitted. "I just didn't know how to ask. You seemed so upset."

Azalea stayed silent for a long moment. But she didn't look away from Ashlyn. It reminded her of that moment back in Merrick's closet, and how vulnerable and exposed it had made her feel.

Finally, Azalea spoke. "The queen takes people."

"What?"

"When it suits her. When the mood strikes. She steals them away. Sometimes they are able to escape. Sometimes they aren't." She swallowed, the bags under her eyes seeming more pronounced. "Sometimes, even if they get out of the castle, it doesn't matter. They can't bring themselves to go on, after all they saw there, all they experienced. Sometimes, they get . . . stuck."

"Stuck . . . Like, stuck sleeping in a tree?"

Ashlyn ventured.

Azalea closed her eyes again. "Yes."

Ashlyn *did* take her hand then. If only in an attempt to remove some of the haunted look on her face. It might have even worked a little. At the very least, Azalea seemed more shocked than tired when she looked at Azalea.

"It's okay," Ashlyn said. "You don't have to tell me anymore. It's okay if it's hard."

Azalea sighed. But she didn't take her hand out of Ashlyn's, and that felt like it meant something. "She won't get to you. I don't care *what* Caul says. We'll . . . We'll be okay."

Ashlyn wasn't sure what to say. She wasn't sure what to think—other than, even through her gloves, the other girl's hand was still very warm. She wasn't sure why she kept noticing that.

"Okay," she said. But even as she spoke, she wasn't sure if it was for her own sake, or for Azalea's.

8

Through The Chessboard

They continued walking, turning and walking in the opposite direction whenever the castle appeared in the distance. When Merrick's booming laugh echoed across the forest, Ashlyn frowned. "Are we back where we started?" She didn't think they'd managed to go back that way, but with all of their turning, she couldn't be sure.

Azalea shook her head. "I doubt it."

They walked forward. The dirt beneath their feet ended, giving way to black and white tile. Standing on those tiles were people, clad in either all black or all white. Some were dressed in leather armor, others in regal clothes, and still others in strange costumes patterned like stone. Their attitudes ranged from happy to bored.

Standing at one end of this display was Lucy. At the other end was Merrick. "Rook to D7!" He shouted. One of the people standing on the tiles walked forward, hands stuffed in the pockets of their strange stone costume. Merrick clapped his hands, laughing. "Checkmate!"

"Rooks can't move diagonal," Lucy objected.

"If he couldn't move there, then how did he get there?" Merrick countered.

Lucy pinched the bridge of her nose. "I don't know why I bother."

Azalea stepped forward. "Are you playing chess?"

Heads turned to look at her—and at Ashlyn. She fought the impulse to step backward, to hide in the trees where she wouldn't make a fuss. Honestly, it was a childish reaction for her to have to a few eyes being on her.

"*I'm* playing chess," Lucy grumbled. "I'm not sure what *Merrick* is playing."

Merrick didn't seem to take offense to the venom in her tone, merely grinning his friendly grin. "Well, perhaps you need a better opponent. Would one of you girls like to try?"

"Don't *we* get a turn?" One of the pieces— Ashlyn thought they were a bishop—muttered to their neighbor.

"Oh, don't sulk," said the knight next to them. "You got to play last week."

"Yes, and Merrick was my king! He

performed a soliloquy after every turn!"

Azalea ignored this byplay, an uncharacteristic softness around her eyes. "I used to *love* chess," she murmured. "Would you mind terribly?"

"Please," Lucy replied. "I'd rather play anyone else."

Merrick abandoned his post eagerly enough, skipping to stand by Ashlyn instead. "How is your search going?" he asked.

Ashlyn frowned, shifting her weight from one foot to the other. "I'm not sure. I don't feel any less confused than when I left your house. If anything, I feel more lost than ever before."

"Well, maybe you need to be more lost before you can be found." Merrick plopped down into the grass, crossing his legs and leaning back on his hands.

Ashlyn looked down at him. "What do you mean?"

"Must everything have meaning?" Merrick asked, eyes sparkling. "Is it not enough for words to be true?"

If this was how Merrick spoke all the time, Ashlyn could understand Lucy's frustration.

She didn't answer, but Merrick seemed undeterred. He gazed down at the grass, cocking his head to the side. "Will you look at that? There's snake grass."

Ashlyn knelt down beside him, examining the ground. "It doesn't look like grass." She plucked a stalk from the ground. The plant had more of the shape of a pine tree branch, but it was a dull brown instead of green. "Why do they call it that?"

"Well, typically, it's green," Merrick explained. "But there's no green left in this forest. No red, either. The queen has stolen it all, hoarded it for herself."

Ashlyn briefly considered the merits of asking how a woman could steal not one but two colors but decided against it. Instead, she looked across the way at Azalea, who was staring at the chessboard. Ashlyn had never seen her look so focused before. Her green eyes were practically glowing.

The queen hadn't managed to steal *all* of that color, then. Something warm and unfamiliar settled between Ashlyn's ribs, curling there like a purring cat.

"Penny for your thoughts?" Merrick asked, and it was only then Ashlyn realized she was smiling.

She rearranged her expression, struck with a terrible urge to change the subject as quickly as possible. "There was someone in the forest looking for snake grass earlier."

"Ah," Merrick said. "You've met Caul, then?"

"You know them?"

"Of course." Merrick shook his head, and for the first time he seemed solemn. "They're one of the few who stay with the queen by choice. I've offered to let them join our merry band of misfits, but they refused."

Ashlyn stared at the snake grass in her hand. She thought of the quiet desperation in their voice when they'd realized it had vanished. Before she knew what she was doing, she was picking another stalk, and another, stuffing them into the pocket of her sweater.

When she looked up, Merrick stared with a curious gleam in his eye. "Hoping to do them a favor?"

"I don't know," Ashlyn responded, which wasn't quite a lie. "Maybe?"

"And what would you ask for in return?"

Ashlyn had no answer for him. Instead, she asked, "Have you ever seen the queen?"

If Merrick thought the change in topic was odd, he didn't say so. "Me? No, I've flown quite under her radar."

"Azalea says she takes people sometimes," Ashlyn murmured. "She said she's . . . awful." The word felt too weak to describe the effect she seemed to have on Azalea, but Ashlyn couldn't think of a better one.

"She would be right in that," Merrick replied. "She's taken plenty over the years. Lucy, for one."

"Lucy?" Suddenly, the darkness around the woman's eyes whenever she spoke of the queen made sense.

"Indeed." Merrick tipped his hat in the direction of the woman in question, still engaged in her chess match. "She spent a few months as a palace knight, mostly fighting other knights for the queen's amusement. It's where she got those scars, you see."

Ashlyn swallowed, something clicking in her throat. Her eyes scanned the scars that littered Lucy's dark skin—the one at her jawline, her collarbone, her arm. She wondered if more littered her body underneath her blouse and flared pants.

"That sounds horrifying," Ashlyn murmured.

"So it is," Merrick agreed. "I suppose I should count myself lucky that she never wanted a court jester."

Ashlyn's gaze drifted across the board to Azalea. She didn't have scars like Lucy, so it seemed unlikely that she'd been a knight. But, then, what *had* the queen done with her? She wasn't sure, but she didn't like any of the possibilities. She found, in fact, that she quite disliked the idea of a hurt Azalea.

She didn't seem hurt now, at least. Far from it. A smile spread across her face like the sunlight breaking through storm clouds. Again came that warmth in Ashlyn's chest, accompanied by a strange fluttering sensation.

"Checkmate," said Azalea.

"Well played." Lucy stretched, rolling her

neck from side to side. "Now, *that* is a loss I'm happy to concede." She shot a very pointed look in Merrick's direction.

Merrick only laughed, throwing his head back in a way that *ought* to have sent his top hat tumbling to the forest floor. Ashlyn supposed that, in the grand scheme of things just lately, a hat that defied the laws of physics was not *so* strange, but it was still a bit disconcerting. "An artist breaks rules," he said, striking a dramatic pose.

Lucy seemed to make an effort to keep a stern face, but it cracked, and she began to giggle into her hands. "You're ridiculous," Merrick blew her a kiss, which she dramatically dodged as though it had physical weight.

Ashlyn caught Azalea's eye. The other girl raised an eyebrow and smiled: a sweet, uncomplicated expression. Ashlyn's chest fluttered again, and she wondered just what it was about Azalea's smile that seemed to elicit this reaction from her. Maybe because it seemed so fragile, so fleeting.

She made her way to the other girl's side, feeling oddly bashful. "Good job," she said.

"Thank you." Azalea touched her own lips, as though surprised by the smile on them. "I had fun. It's a little surprising . . . I thought I'd lost the energy for puzzles like this. I suppose I have you to thank for that."

Ashlyn blinked. "Me?"

"You." Azalea shook her head. "With all your talk of finding a way out of here. It made me remember . . . the way I used to think. The way I used to *feel*." She smiled. The exhaustion didn't vanish from her eyes, but it did seem more distant somehow. "What is this forest, after all, if not a puzzle?"

"Maybe . . . Maybe that's a good way to look at it." Ashlyn's hand found its way into her pocket, touching the snake grass. If the forest *was* a puzzle, was this a piece of it?

Before she could say anything about that, a low snarl broke through the forest.

The chess pieces all cried out and scattered, some of them shedding more cumbersome costumes as they went. Ashlyn looked around just in time to catch Merrick vanishing into the trees.

"What was that?" she asked.

"The wolves," Lucy murmured. Her eyes were dark. "You girls need to run." And with that, she took her own advice, vanishing after Merrick.

Azalea took Ashlyn by the hand. "Come on."

Ashlyn, who remembered the wolves quite well, needed no further encouragement. They broke into a sprint just as the creatures skidded into view, jaws dripping with saliva.

- 9 -

Through The Hollow

Once, Ashlyn had been caught outside in a horrible storm. The sky had turned a sickly yellow, and the threatening howl of the wind had not been loud enough to obscure the whine of the tornado siren as it cut through the air. Ashlyn had run with her shoulders hunched against flying branches and debris, nerves turned to live wires by sheer helpless fear.

Running from the wolves was a bit like that. But unlike when she'd fled from the tornado, there was no home waiting for her at the end of it, no father to sweep her up into his arms and carry her into the basement where she would be safe, scolding her in the sort of trembling voice that belied his fear. There was only running, and running, and more running.

Except that wasn't quite true. There was Azalea.

As they ran, she didn't let go of Ashlyn's hand, not once. And although Azalea ran a little slow, her steps just a bit clumsy, Ashlyn kept clinging, as well. It was comforting to know that even though she was fleeing, she wasn't fleeing alone.

"There!" Azalea hissed, pointing. It took Ashlyn a moment before she realized what she was pointing at—a hole in the earth, so overgrown with branches that it was almost invisible. It would be the perfect place to hide, a sanctuary every bit as reasonable as the basement she once fled to.

But the sight of it didn't fill Ashlyn with relief. Far from it. Her heart pounded, her breath catching in her throat. She did *not* want to go into that hole. If not for Azalea's hand still clamped around her wrist, she would have kept running.

But Azalea's hand *was* still on her wrist, and Azalea was dragging her toward the hole. Ashlyn didn't want to argue with her, not when she didn't have a good reason for feeling so frightened and not when she could hear the wolves crashing through the trees. She allowed Azalea to lead her.

They pressed into the hollow, the scent of damp earth surrounding them. It should have been comforting, hidden away from the wolves as they prowled past, but it wasn't. It *wasn't*. Something in this hollow space was bad, wrong, *dangerous*.

Azalea shifted her weight, jostling Ashlyn further in. Earth hit her back as she reached the end of the hollow, and she instinctively tried to flinch away from the chill of it. But she couldn't move. The earth sucked her in, all darkness and dampness and rot. Her vision tunneled and her head spun, the view of the forest outside getting smaller and further away, as if she were falling.

Only that didn't make any sense. Outside was in front of her, not above her. Or was it? Could she be sure of anything anymore?

Ashlyn tried to cry out. She tried to move. But she couldn't. All she could do was lay there with the damp earth at her back and the stench of rot surrounding her. This wasn't right. This wasn't *right*. She couldn't breathe, couldn't think. What was she doing here? Why wasn't anyone coming to help her?

"I think the wolves are gone," a voice said from somewhere far off. "We should be okay to get out . . . Ashlyn?"

Ashlyn blinked, struggling to focus. Someone was here with her. Someone.

Azalea?

As if summoned by her thoughts, Azalea appeared, frowning in the opening of the hole. The opening, which was exactly as close as it had been before. Ashlyn scrambled out, collapsing to her hands and knees in the dirt.

She was free.

But what had *happened* back there? And why was it still so hard for her to breathe?

"Ashlyn!" Hands were on her back. Distantly, she realized they were Azalea's. "Ashlyn, it's okay. Breathe. In . . . and out."

Ashlyn Jones was an obedient child, but even as obedient as she was, she found obeying this command particularly difficult. Still, she tried. But after a few tries, it came a little easier. Then a little easier still.

Sense returned to her slowly, swimming back to her as if coming out of some horrible nightmare. Her heart rate slowed, leaving only a strange metallic taste in the back of her throat. She became aware that at some point she had curled up on the ground, knees drawn up to her stomach and forehead pressed against the earth. She arranged herself into more of a sitting position, although it took longer before she could bring herself to uncurl her body from its protective ball.

Azalea, still at her side, put a cautious hand on her back. "Are you feeling better?"

"Yes. I—I'm sorry, I don't, I *don't* . . ." Ashlyn trailed off, waving a trembling hand vaguely instead of finishing her sentence.

"That's alright." Azalea's voice was so gentle. "Ashlyn . . . have you had a panic attack before?"

A panic attack? Had that been what that was? Ashlyn wasn't sure, but she supposed it made sense. Although she'd never experienced anything quite that intense, she was prone to worrying herself into stomach aches or tears over even little things. It was something her mother would often roll her eyes at. *Oh, stop that,* she'd scold. *You're getting worked up over nothing.* She'd learned to keep it to herself.

Only this time, she hadn't quite managed that.

Her cheeks burned. "I'm sorry," she murmured.

Azalea studied her face, as if considering something. When she spoke, her voice was very gentle. "Would you like a hug?"

Ashlyn considered this for a moment. She was no longer gasping for air, but she did still feel very raw, and very fragile, and quite scared. More than a little sheepishly, she nodded.

Azalea wrapped her arms around Ashlyn carefully, as if afraid of spooking her. It helped, and the mere fact that it helped made Ashlyn feel embarrassed all over again. "I really am sorry," she said. "You shouldn't have had to deal with that. I'm sorry for being so difficult, when you're already going out of your way to help me."

Azalea pulled away, if only to make eye contact. "You clearly didn't do it on purpose. I won't hold it against you. That would be cruel."

That didn't strike Ashlyn as correct. Her parents scolded her for doing things on accident all the time. That was how she learned. She was *supposed* to apologize whenever her silly fears or strange thoughts caused trouble for other people. That was the way it was supposed to go.

But Azalea didn't look at her like she needed to apologize. Ashlyn wasn't really sure what to do with that.

"Well, thank you, then," she finally said. "Even if I wasn't much help there."

"I wouldn't say that," Azalea said, her gaze turning thoughtful. "I'm glad I had you with me. I don't know if I would have escaped the wolves in the first place otherwise."

"What? Why?"

Azalea frowned. "I'm not very good at running," she said, in a tone that made it sound like she meant something else entirely.

Ashlyn wasn't really sure what that something was. She just knew that it made her want to hug Azalea again. Instead, she cleared her throat. "Well, I'm glad you didn't," she said. "I'd be sad if you got eaten by wolves."

Azalea laughed then. It wasn't a happy laugh, but neither was it a sad one. It was, maybe, a bit relieved, as though she'd turned around and found out that the stranger stalking her home had been her own shadow all along.

"Yeah," Azalea said, almost wondering. "Me, too."

10

Through The Pathways

After an indeterminate length of time, Ashlyn stood. "We should keep going."

Azalea startled, as if woken from a dream. "Of course." She stood, but she moved slowly, stiffly.

Ashlyn frowned. Now that she wasn't so jittery with nerves, she noticed how tense Azalea was holding herself, the tightness in her jaw and the rapidness of her breath. She was frightened. Ashlyn went to her, hovering cautiously in her orbit. "Are you alright?"

"I'm fine." Azalea shook out her wrists, then her hair, as if trying to rid herself of a bug. "I just hope those wolves don't come back, is all."

"They *are* scary." The wolves hadn't given

her a panic attack, but that didn't mean she had enjoyed their presence. "You fought them before, though."

"That was different," Azalea said. "More the tree than me."

"Did you hear me at all?"

Azalea's gaze went distant. "There might have been a part of me that was . . . listening. Looking for someone to listen *to*. But I don't think it's something I could repeat now, even if given that power. I hadn't been awake enough to be afraid, then."

Ashlyn wasn't sure how to take that. "Are you . . . upset that I woke you?"

Azalea focused on her then, her smile turning soft. "No. *No*. It's better to feel fear than to feel nothing at all. You can trust me on that." She shook her head, looking off in the distance with a small expression of distaste. "Fear is the proper response, anyway. Those wolves are horrid."

"Where do you think they come from?" Ashlyn mused.

"Oh." Azalea blinked. "I don't think. I know. They come from the queen."

Of course. Ashlyn frowned, looking down the path. How long would it take for the castle to appear in the distance, forcing them to turn and lose what little momentum they had? "I don't like it," she murmured. "What are we supposed to do? Just wander aimlessly, waiting for another one of her threats? What if she's already looking for us, what if that's why those wolves are out?"

"I don't like it, either." Azalea looked even paler than usual at the thought. "But I don't think we have any other options. If we go to the castle, the queen *will* catch us."

"And what happens if we don't? We fumble around until she catches us anyway?" Ashlyn could hear her own voice growing harsher than she intended, edged with desperation. She didn't mean to sound that way, but she couldn't seem to help it, either.

Azalea slumped in on herself. She looked, suddenly, very small. "I don't know what else to do. *Is* there anything else to do? Or will we just . . ." She trailed off, staring into the trees. Finally, she sighed. "I just don't know."

"Neither do I," Ashlyn said. "But we have to try something." She slipped her hand into her pocket. The snake grass was still there. "I have an idea."

Azalea turned to her, eyes tired but with a certain focus in them nonetheless. "What is it?"

Ashlyn pulled out the snake grass from her pocket. "This is what Caul was looking for earlier. If we find them and use it to bargain, maybe they'll help us get through the castle unnoticed. We can look around, at least."

"You still think the way out is through the castle." Azalea's tone was curiously flat.

"I think it's the only thing that makes any *sense*. If all paths lead there, that has to mean something." Ashlyn fought to keep her voice calm. She didn't want to yell at Azalea—her frustration didn't have anything to do with Azalea, really. "I know what you said before, but . . . how can you be *sure* that there isn't a way out hiding in there somewhere?"

"I suppose I don't have a good answer to that." Azalea pressed the heels of her palms to her eyes. "Goodness, but this is horrendous. Do you understand how dangerous what you're suggesting is?"

"I . . . I do. Maybe not in the same way you do, but I do. I've seen the wolves. And I've heard the stories. It's frightening." She touched the back of Azalea's hand, trying to be gentle. "But, Azalea, I don't think we're any safer here in this forest. This could be our only option."

Azalea looked down at her hand, wavy brown hair covering her face. "The others seem to be existing comfortably enough. But . . . that doesn't hold any appeal to you, does it?"

"No."

"Because you want to go home."

"I . . ." Ashlyn trailed off, although she wasn't quite sure why. Azalea was right—she did want to go home. That was why she was fighting so hard to get out of this forest, wasn't it? All she'd wanted from the beginning was for things to go back to normal.

But then she thought about picking out her own clothes. Or Azalea comforting her instead of scolding her. It wasn't that she didn't want to see her parents again. It wasn't that she wanted to run away. And she definitely didn't want to stay in the forest. It was just that . . . the idea of going back home felt different, now.

She wasn't sure how to vocalize any of that to Azalea, though. So instead she said, "I don't like feeling trapped," which was a perfectly true sentiment and still got her point across. She didn't want to remain in this forest forever. That was what she'd focus on.

Azalea looked down, her expression as soft as her voice. "I understand."

Ashlyn took her hand then. She couldn't explain why, but it felt like the most natural thing to do in that moment. "If you don't want to join me, I won't blame you," she said. "I've appreciated having you here so far, but I won't force you to come along on this."

Azalea looked up, eyes widening slightly. "No, I . . . I'll stay with you." She smiled. It wasn't quite as bright as the one she'd given at the chess match, but there was something genuine about it all the same. "It's frightening, true, but . . . I can't help but admire your determination."

" . . . Oh." Ashlyn had expected her to be harder to convince. "Well, thank you." She pulled the other girl to her feet, a fire in her chest. "Now, all we have to do is find Caul."

As if summoned, Caul turned the corner onto the path, brushing dirt off of their large cloak.

Azalea began to laugh. It sounded better than before, but only slightly. "Oh, but this place has a sick sense of humor sometimes."

Caul froze mid-swipe at the fabric, staring at them both. "Hello," they said. "I don't suppose you two know which way the palace is this time? I'm running late, and the queen will be cross with me for not finding the snake grass but she'll be even *more* cross with me if I'm late for dinner, so . . ."

Ashlyn cleared her throat. "I can't help with the second. But as for the first . . ." Before she could lose her nerve, she pulled the snake grass out of her pocket.

The moment Caul saw the snake grass pinched between Ashlyn's fingers, their eyes widened. They lurched forward with the sort of raw energy that Ashlyn associated with drowning. "Give me that."

Surprising even herself, Ashlyn stepped away from them, holding the snake grass out of reach. "I can do that! But you'll need to do something for me."

Caul gave her a wary look. Ashlyn could feel Azalea staring at her, too, but she didn't take her eyes off of the cloaked figure in front of her. Her heart pounded in her chest, and she *knew* she was being terribly rude. But there were more important things than being polite.

"If I go to the castle," she said, "will you help me investigate it without the queen noticing?"

"What?" Caul swiped for the snake grass again, letting out a frustrated groan when Ashlyn again stepped out of their range. "You're crazy."

"Can you help, or not?"

Caul rolled their eyes. "Give me a few hours' head start. Meet me at the gates of the palace. I'll offer you something to cloak yourself . . . but that's all I'm offering you. I can't give you any sort of guarantee that it will work."

The offer didn't exactly inspire confidence. But it was *something*, and right now, something was exactly what they needed. Ashlyn handed over the snake grass.

"Deal."

11

Through The Meadow

With Caul off preparing, the girls were left with nothing to do but wait.

Loitering on the path wasn't an appealing option, especially with the wolves still out there somewhere. But after a bit of walking, they came upon a field where the grass rolled in dark brown hills, the castle on the horizon bright against the dusk. Ashlyn thought there was little chance for the wolves to sneak up on them in such a wide-open space.

Azalea seemed to think the same, because she laid down in the grass, her brown hair framing her face like a halo. Ashlyn sat beside her, expecting it to feel brittle to the touch. But although it was brown as though it were dying, it felt as soft as velvet.

It felt good to sit. It occurred to Ashlyn that she should have gotten tired by now. Tired and hungry. Then again, how long *had* it been since she fell? Could she really be sure? "I think the way the sky never changes is starting to mess with me," she said.

"I'd say you get used to it, but I'm not sure that's true. Maybe it's better to say you grow numb to it, but . . ." Azalea sighed, her voice dropping to a confessional whisper. "I miss the stars."

Ashlyn looked up. The dusk sky was, still, *just* too bright for stars. Something about the sight of it, or maybe just the longing in Azalea's tone, made her heart ache. Laying down beside the other girl, she tilted her head just slightly, catching her profile in her gaze. "What else do you miss?"

Azalea closed her eyes for a moment, as though she meant to sleep. But then she spoke, spoke with a voice that ached, weighted down with every moment she had spent in this place. "*Everything*. Even little things. Birds singing in the morning. The smell of freshly baked bread. Coming across one of my favorite flowers on a walk. I hadn't realized how much I would miss it. I hadn't realized how much I would miss *all* of it. I wish I would have . . . I wish I *could* have appreciated it all more."

She sounded near tears, and Ashlyn almost regretted asking. But she also didn't. Because the ache in the other girl's voice seemed necessary somehow. Ashlyn rolled on her side to face her. "It's not your fault. You didn't mean to end up here, right? You just got lost, like the rest of us."

Azalea opened her eyes, turning to Ashlyn. For a moment, it felt like the forest dropped away, and there were just those *eyes*. The only green in this place that didn't belong to the castle and its notorious ruler.

"What will you do," Azalea asked, "once you *do* find the end of this forest?"

The question gave Ashlyn pause, far more so than it would have at the beginning of all this. She turned back up to the sky, as though she could find the answer there if she looked hard enough. But, as Azalea so sadly noted, there were no stars to chart her course by. She was on her own.

"It's difficult to say," she admitted. "I do want to go back. I miss my bed, I miss my home, I miss my parents. And I'm sure they're very worried about me. But . . ."

"But?"

Ashlyn paused, thinking through her words carefully before she spoke. "My mother calls me her little doll. It's meant to be a fond nickname, I know, but the more I think about it, the more I wonder . . . is that all I am to her?" She laughed. "I suppose I sound very dramatic."

"Be dramatic, then." There was a small

smile in Azalea's voice. "I wouldn't deny you that."

"But that's it! Back home, it isn't like that. I can't be too dramatic or too uncaring, too loud or too quiet, too upset or too happy. My parents pick out the clothes I wear, the people I see. I've hidden so much of myself—*so* much of myself—all to please them. And I don't know if I want to go back to that. I don't know if I *can*."

Azalea was quiet. When Ashlyn turned, she was looking at her, all wide green eyes and pale, solemn face. She looked ethereal, somehow, as though lit by the very stars she missed so dearly. When she spoke, her voice was almost drowned out by the sound of the wind in the grass.

"What would you be instead?"

"I'm not sure," Ashlyn admitted. "But I'd like to find out. I *will* find out." She looked up at the sky, reaching up to the blue-gray as though she could pull the future closer with her own two hands. "When I get back home, things are going to be different. I'll stand up for myself. I'll wear what I want to wear, even if Mom says it looks silly. I'll do what I want to do, even if Dad says its unbecoming. I'll do . . . Everything. Anything."

She could see it now. A future that stretched before her, bright and endless. A life she could live instead of passively endure, a life where there was so much more to experience than the fleeting moments of joy she could find within the confines of her parents' plans for her.

Azalea had gone quiet again. When Ashlyn looked at her, she seemed pensive, but her face broke into a smile when she saw Ashlyn's gaze catch her own.

"That sounds," she said, "very nice."

It occurred to her, then, that Azalea's face was really quite close to her own. It occurred to her, as well, that Azalea's face was beautiful. The thought clicked into place with the sort of clarity that couldn't be taken back. It was as though she'd been staring at an optical illusion for hours, only to suddenly see the picture hidden behind the patterns and lines.

Azalea was beautiful, and her face was close, and Ashlyn wanted to kiss her.

The thought was startling, but not new. Like her anger, like her fear, like a thousand other things, she had pushed it down. It wasn't as though her parents ever said outright that she wasn't allowed to find women attractive. They didn't have to. She knew, just from how they spoke, that they saw a husband and children in her future. That was what they wanted.

But what they wanted wasn't important. What Ashlyn wanted was.

But what Azalea wanted was important, too. If Ashlyn kissed her, would Azalea kiss her back? Was the too-small distance between them purposeful, did Azalea *want* her to close it? Or was Ashlyn the only one hyper-aware of just how close they were?

Ashlyn studied Azalea's face, looking for any sort of hint. But this was not the sort of emotion that she had experience with. She hadn't the faintest idea what she was even looking for, and the fact that she suddenly found the curve of Azalea's lips *very* distracting did not help matters.

Her heart pounded; her pulse raced. She moved forward slightly, not closing the distance so much as chipping away at it. Azalea sat up, turning the narrow gap between them into a chasm.

"I suppose Caul will be ready by now," she said.

Was this a polite rejection, or a misunderstanding? Ashlyn couldn't be sure, and it wasn't as though she could just come out and *ask* about it. Or, well, she could—she did not think that Azalea would be the type to be cruel to her, even if turning her down. But Azalea was right. They had more important things to focus on.

So, ignoring the slight sting in her heart (and it really *was* slight), Ashlyn sat up. "Let's go, then."

12

Through The Hedges

The castle seemed to grow larger all too quickly, as though it were moving toward them with the same speed they moved toward it. Red stone towers slashed the night sky like an open wound, their jagged edges calling to mind the gaping maw of some predator. Before it, rows of green hedges seemed to almost slither like serpents.

Beside Ashlyn, Azalea made a quiet noise. Ashlyn did not have to be a mind reader to see the fear in her eyes, or the anxiety in her gait. "Are you sure you want to do this?" she asked. "I wouldn't judge if you wanted to wait out here for me."

Azalea appeared to seriously consider this prospect for a long moment. But then, slowly, she shook her head. "No. I want to stay with you."

Ashlyn's heart fetched up against her ribs, stumbling in its steady rhythm. Impulsively, she reached out, taking the other girl's hand in hers. "It will be okay."

Azalea smiled, some of that fear draining from her expression. And, for a moment, Ashlyn thought that her cheeks might have turned a light pink. Maybe that hadn't been a refusal, back in the grass—or if it had been, it was one of nervousness and not dislike.

Well. There would be time to figure all of that out once this was over with.

The castle grew closer, then closer, then closer still. Red spires grew large enough to blot out the sky. Trees gave way to hedges, clipped in the neat sort of walls that reminded Ashlyn a little too much of her parents' home.

Caul waited there in front of the rows of greenery. Their eyes darted around beneath the hood of their cloak, and every few seconds they turned to look behind them, as though expecting the queen to materialize in the hedges. Which wasn't, Ashlyn had to concede, an impossibility. She really knew very little about what the queen was actually capable of. Her chest twisted uncomfortably at the thought as Caul frowned at her.

"I can't stay long," they said. "Here." They held out two necklaces, each with a pendant that seemed to disappear and reappear as the silver chains swung. "These will make you unnoticeable."

Ashlyn took the necklace and put it on. When she turned, Azalea had already fastened the clasp on her own necklace, and she stood with her hands wound tightly together. Ashlyn looked back to Caul. "I don't understand? I can still see her."

"It doesn't make you invisible, it makes you unnoticeable," Caul explained. "So long as you don't announce your presence or make it obvious, you'll be fine. People will overlook you. Most people, anyway." They glanced over their shoulder. "I'd try to stay out of the queen's line of sight, if I were you. I can't say for sure how well these will work against her."

Ashlyn took a deep breath. This was frightening, but she'd gone too far to turn back now. She turned to Azalea, putting on what she hoped was a brave face. "Are you ready?"

Azalea nodded. "Ready."

Knowing that Azalea was with her made her feel a little bit better. She turned to face Caul, but they'd already disappeared. Ashlyn frowned. "They're almost as impatient as Kazuo."

This made Azalea laugh. Ashlyn felt even better.

After so long surrounded by the burnt oranges and browns of the forest, the vivid green hedges were almost blinding. Ashlyn squinted against them, hand instinctively going up to shield her eyes. "Is it just me, or is even the sky here brighter?"

The sky still seemed to be its normal dusk color. But the leaves didn't look the way leaves ought to look at night, dull and devoid of sunlight. They reflected invisible light in disorienting patterns.

Azalea only shrugged. Her body language was still too tense, her lips pressed tightly together. Again, Ashlyn thought about offering to let her turn around, but she'd already made her position clear. It felt wrong to push, even when the other girl was so clearly uncomfortable.

They went deeper into the hedges. They weren't truly a maze so much as they were a pathway, but Ashlyn's head still spun faintly. Every once in a while, the branches would creak and shuffle, as though they were only forming the tunnels as fast as she and Azalea could walk through them.

They stepped out into a wide clearing dominated by the castle. It towered higher than any building Ashlyn had ever seen, bright red walls shining as though made of polished stone. Two guards sat on the front steps, both clothed in silver armor. Neither of them seemed particularly interested in guarding, however. One sat hunched over their own knees, trembling, while the other hovered over them, a hand on their shoulder.

"I can't do this anymore," the hunched-over one said in a small, quavering voice. "I can't fight anymore, I can't, I can't."

"It will be okay," the second said. "The wounds never last, you know that. They scar over quickly, there's no real damage done."

"But they hurt," the first wailed. "And anywhere else, you can at least stop if you get injured enough. Here, you're only done when the queen's decided she's seen enough blood."

Ashlyn's stomach turned. Even as they walked through the castle doors, opening them as slowly and quietly as possible to avoid detection, the memory of the guard's sobs followed her. Not to mention the memory of Lucy's scars.

Azalea let out a quiet, heavy noise. "It doesn't feel right, does it?"

"What?" Ashlyn asked.

"Leaving them like that." Azalea's frown was distant, lost in thought. "Maybe we could have told them about Lucy and the others. The ones who escaped. Given them some hope."

That was a good idea. Good in the sense that it was kind, anyway, but perhaps not good in the sense that it was wise. "Caul told us to keep a low profile," Ashlyn reminded her. "We've got a job to do here."

Azalea shifted her weight, glancing over her

shoulder. But, in the end, she sighed. "Right. Let's go on."

The forest was strange, and the hedges more so. But the castle made both of them seem perfectly ordinary. The rooms seemed to have a strangely malleable quality, and Ashlyn found herself forgetting what she had seen in one hallway once she'd walked to the next. It was sort of like being in a dream, where everything had a fuzzy, disconnected quality.

"I forgot how awful this feels," Azalea murmured.

They stepped into a room. It seemed somehow more solid than the hallways, with high ceilings and pillared archways. A long, narrow rug ran from the door to the back wall, where a sparkling throne sat.

"This is the queen's, right?" Ashlyn asked.

"Yes," Azalea replied. Her voice trembled. "Ashlyn, I don't think we should be in here."

"Wait." There was something about the throne—or, rather, the wall behind it. There was a seam to it, something that looked like ornamentation until Ashlyn squinted.

"Azalea, is that a door behind the throne?"

It was. Ashlyn swore it was. But before she could investigate, a shadow fell over them from behind. A feminine voice, quiet but powerful, echoed through the throne room.

"Goodness. Now, this is a surprise."

13

Through The Throne Room

The castle had never felt more dreamlike than it did when Ashlyn turned to behold the queen.

It was strange. For all Ashlyn had heard of the queen's personality, she hadn't given much thought to what she *looked* like. Whatever her preconceived notions had been, the woman standing before her didn't match them.

The queen was tall. Not unusually so, but enough that she had to look down her upturned nose at Ashlyn and Azalea, her blue eyes framed by thick eyelashes. She had an elegant, heart-shaped face, her cheeks dusted over with blush and her lips the same vivid red as her dress. Her hair was gold and twisted into an intricate hairstyle. She reminded Ashlyn a little of movie stars in photos from red carpet events, her beauty just this side of impossible.

A golden crown glittered on her head, but even without it, Ashlyn wouldn't have doubted her identity. The queen had an aura, a *pull* unlike anything in the natural world. Even as she stepped forward, leaving the exit wide open, Ashlyn remained rooted to the spot. The throne room's walls seemed to warp as the queen passed through them, as though bowing.

"What on earth are you doing here, Azalea?" The queen's voice was as surprising as the rest of her: warm and almost *friendly*, as though Azalea was an unexpected companion who had dropped in for tea. "I must say, you're the last person I expected to see. I thought you grew tired of my court."

"Wait," Ashlyn said. "You *let* her go?"

"*Let* her . . . goodness!" The queen laughed, high and chiming like a bell. "What sort of stories have you been telling about me?"

"Don't listen to her," Azalea muttered to Ashlyn, voice trembling.

Ashlyn squared her shoulders, trying to sound brave. "You don't fool me. You can act friendly, but I've seen what you did to Lucy. To your knights." *To Azalea,* she thought, but didn't say. Partially because she still wasn't sure what scarred Azalea so, and partially because she didn't want to draw any more attention to the other girl than necessary. Although the necklaces seemed to be worthless against the queen, the general sentiment still seemed wise.

The queen hummed. "*Lucy*. Now there's a name I haven't heard in awhile. She was a *fabulous* fighter. Lost every match! I think it was her way of taking a stand—refusing to play. So noble, although I wonder very much if her fellow knights deserved that kindness. They were, after all, the ones spilling her blood all over my arena. Oh, and what *lovely* blood it was."

She shared this final sentiment with the same easy cheer she'd greeted them with. Ashlyn shivered. "You're mad," she blurted.

"Well, I always thought that was rather a matter of perspective," the queen replied. "In a mad kingdom full of mad people, one could argue that it's really quite *sane* for me to be mad. Logical, even, if you think about it."

Ashlyn felt sick. The queen's tone reminded her a little of Merrick's ramblings, but with none of his charm. "It . . . okay, that isn't the point. The problem isn't that you're mad. It's that you hurt people. I've heard what you do, it's . . . it's evil."

"Oh, goodness, well. You sound very sure of yourself, so I suppose you must be right." The queen clasped her hands at her waist, her wide eyes almost disarmingly guileless. "Tell me, then. If you know everything, and if I'm so very wicked, then what are you doing here in my castle?"

"I . . ." Ashlyn trailed off. She certainly couldn't tell the queen the truth. Then again, what *was* the truth? Even she wasn't sure what she was searching for. She glanced toward the throne, sure that she had seen *something* behind it. But it seemed blurry and indistinct now, and she could no longer quite remember what it was she had noticed before.

Ashlyn turned to Azalea. At least she was solid. Azalea stared back at her for a moment, then surprised her by stepping forward. "Your knights," she murmured. "I wanted to help them. I wanted to free them. That's why we're here."

"Oh, how fun!" The queen clapped her hands together once. "What a charming tale. So creative, too. You always *did* have an interesting way of looking at the world, Azalea. Not that you did much with it! A bit wasteful, if you ask me."

Azalea's face crumpled, but she stood firm. "Your court—"

"Oh, dear, enough about the court." The queen waved an errant hand. "No doubt your sweet little heart bleeds for them, but planning a rescue? That isn't your style, darling. You and I both know you don't have the vision to pull something like that off. To say nothing of the energy!"

Azalea looked away, hands curling into fists. She didn't say anything, and Ashlyn wasn't sure what to say on her behalf. This conversation had taken on a strange, almost dreamlike lilt. The spaces between words bulged with all of the things Ashlyn didn't know—all of the things she hadn't been able to bring herself to press Azalea on. She had never, in all of her time in this place, felt more out of her depth.

"No, darling," the queen continued. "This has nothing to do with my court. We both know that you're only making up a story of heroics to protect Ashlyn."

Ashlyn gasped. "How do you know my name?"

"Oh, I know a good many things about you." The queen drifted toward her throne, her skirts moving in great sweeping movements. "I knew you from the moment you fell. You're a special case, my dear. I thought for a while that Azalea would be the one to do it, but she was as disappointing as all the others. Now I see it, though. It's you. It's *always* been you."

The queen's eyes shone. Ashlyn wasn't sure what to make of it. "If you know so much, shouldn't you know why I'm here already? Is this just another game for you?"

"You're so much more important than a game," the queen replied. "I knew you would come, that is true. But a 'why' is hard to come by in this place, as I'm sure you've found." She leaned forward in her seat, hands laced beneath her chin. "So, humor me. What *are* you doing here?"

Ashlyn looked to Azalea, but this time there was no help—only her own frightened and tense gaze mirrored back to her in green. Ashlyn became suddenly sure that the queen would catch her in a lie. That only left the truth.

"I want to go home," Ashlyn said. "And I think the way out is through this castle."

She expected many things from the queen upon this proclamation, but the queen did the strangest thing of all: she laughed. She laughed long and hard, bent over with the force of it. The sound of her laughter filled the room like quicksand, trapping them within. Ashlyn almost expected to go to her knees with the force of it.

"Oh, but you are a silly one, aren't you?" The queen wiped at her eyes. "That is the funniest joke I have ever heard."

"I—I'm not joking." Ashlyn swallowed, trying and failing to keep the tremble from her voice. "The way out is here, isn't it? You're hiding it."

The queen looked at her inquisitively. The mirth in her face died out in sections, leaving behind a blank watchfulness more unnerving than any affectation that had come before.

"You aren't kidding," the queen said, more statement than question. "Then could it be that you don't know? I knew you wouldn't right away, of course, you're too special, but . . ." She turned to Azalea then, horribly curious. "You didn't tell her?"

"Tell me what?" Ashlyn looked to Azalea, but there was no green gaze to meet hers. Azalea stared at the floor, trembling. "Azalea, tell me *what*?"

"Oh, you poor thing. I'm sorry I laughed at you." The horrible thing was, the queen *sounded* sorry. "I thought you must know."

"What are you talking about?"

The queen stood then, approaching Ashlyn with careful steps. Her gaze wavered between pity and curiosity, a hideous combination that made Ashlyn feel like a bug caught under the microscope.

"You can't go home," the queen said, "because you're dead. You died when you fell down that well. This, my dear, is what comes next."

14

Through The Castle

You're dead.

Ashlyn wanted to reject those words outright. To call them ridiculous, as mad as anything else in this twisted kingdom. But the statement didn't elicit the emotions it ought to have, surprised incredulousness melting into indignant refusal.

Because Ashlyn remembered. Oh, god, she *remembered*. How could she have ever forgotten?

The wood collapsing beneath her weight. The tumble into darkness, into dampness, into a rotting hole in the earth. Stinking water clogging her nose, her throat. Limbs bent at impossible angles, limbs she couldn't move. Cold seeping into every inch of her, carving into her like knives.

It all returned to her, the same panic that had seized her when she'd hidden from the wolves. Only now she understood that it hadn't been just a hallucination—it had been a *memory*. How long had she laid, paralyzed and half-drowning? Minutes, hours? Days, even? Ashlyn couldn't be sure. There had been no room in her for anything but raw, animal panic, and then not even that.

And now she was here. And she was screaming. A hand was patting her back gently, and it took several moments before Ashlyn could register that hand as belonging to the queen.

"I'm sorry you had to find out this way."

Ashlyn drew in a breath. Another. She was breathing—wasn't she? Could she really be sure of anything anymore? "I can't be dead," she said. "I can't, it's not—you don't understand, my whole life, I wasn't—I didn't do it *right*. I can see that now. I was going to fix everything, so why—why is this *happening* to me?"

Her voice broke. Her thoughts turned to, of all things, the kids at the roller rink. Why hadn't she gone back to them? She could have walked there if she'd tried, if she hadn't cared so much what her father would think. And then she wouldn't have . . . she wouldn't have . . .

"It isn't *fair*," Ashlyn wailed.

"I knew you'd understand." The queen's

voice was horribly gentle. "You know what it's like. You're special."

Ashlyn didn't feel special, not in that moment. To say that she felt *sad* would be to compare a hurricane to a breeze; to say that she felt *scared* would be to compare a decapitation to a paper cut. Ashlyn felt sick, and hurt, and beyond all that, she felt *cheated*. It was an emotion that was so much bigger than anger, but it still led to the same.

Ashlyn rounded on Azalea with wide, burning eyes. "Is it true? Did you know all along?"

She wanted, desperately, to believe it wasn't true. But Azalea's face told a different story. Her eyes were too wide, her skin too pale. Her bottom lip trembled as her hands curled, nails digging into her palms.

"I . . . I knew," she said. "I knew it all along. Everyone is dead here. Even you. Even me."

In other circumstances, that final admission would have elicited more sympathy from Ashlyn. But there was no room in her heart for sympathy. It was too full of terror, of grief, of the memories of her dying alone in the dark.

"*Why*?" The word ached as it tore its way from Ashlyn's throat. "Why wouldn't you tell me? Why help me—and all that talk about my future, why would you say that if it was all *worthless*?"

Azalea was the one who asked her what she

would do, if given the chance. Azalea was the one who helped her realize that she'd been living her life for other people instead of herself. Why would she do that? What was the *point* of realizing how to live better if she couldn't live at all?

"You hoped." Azalea stared down at the polished red floor. "Hope. I couldn't bring myself to take that from you. It would have been too cruel."

Hands descended onto Ashlyn's shoulders. The queen stood behind her, her strange presence palpable even out of sight. "Liars often claim they're being kind," she murmured. "But we know the truth, don't we, special girl?"

Ashlyn turned to face her. "You keep saying I'm special. What do you mean by that?"

"I mean, life was terribly unfair to you." The queen stroked a hand through Ashlyn's hair. The touch didn't feel comforting, not exactly, but it did feel solid, and it made Ashlyn feel a bit more solid in turn. More *present*. She did not back away as the queen gazed upon her with those bright blue eyes. "You died before you could truly live. You had everything stolen from you. But all is not lost."

"I don't understand," Ashlyn whispered.

"Join my court," the queen said. "Not as a knight or a servant, but as a princess."

"Ashlyn, don't do it," Azalea pleaded. Ashlyn did not look at her. Her gaze remained fixed on the queen, whose serene expression looked more and more sane by the moment. Maybe it *was* all about perspective.

"You won't make me fight?"

"I won't make you do anything. You've had enough of that, haven't you?"

"Then, will I become like you? Will I become . . ." She trailed off, unsure of what to say. She'd called the queen *evil* before. But she was no longer sure that word fit. "Bloodthirsty?"

"You may." The queen offered a smile. "You'll find that power corrupts in strange ways. You won't be the same girl you were, but that's not such a hardship. You wanted to change, didn't you?"

"I . . . I did." That much, she couldn't deny. "But I don't think I want to become . . . cruel."

"Are you sure it matters?" The queen shrugged, disarmingly casual. "If you *do* become cruel, it's not as though you will care about such things anymore. And everyone here is already dead, so you don't have to worry about doing any lasting damage to them."

Ashlyn turned and looked at Azalea. Azalea, who had saved her life. Azalea, who had offered to help her again and again. Azalea, who was beautiful. Azalea, who part of her had wanted to kiss back in that meadow.

Azalea, who she had trusted.

Azalea, who had lied to her.

Ashlyn turned and faced the queen. "I'll do it."

"Ashlyn, no!" Azalea stepped forward, but a line of knights marched in, blocking her from going any further. Unlike the knights on the steps, they wore their helmets, standing straight and anonymous. Snarling wolves flanked several of them, and Azalea cowered.

Ashlyn didn't cower. She tilted her head up, willing her voice steady. "The queen is right. I don't care if I become cruel. Why should I care? The world didn't care if it was cruel to *me*. At least this way, I get . . . I get . . ."

She didn't know how to finish that statement. This seemed like the right decision, operating under the same strange dream logic that had dictated so much of her journey here. But explaining herself felt impossible. Everything about this was impossible.

Was it any wonder that everyone in this strange kingdom was mad?

"Take her away," she whispered to the guards. And as they obeyed, something terrible and powerful swelled in her chest.

15

Through The Ballroom

he queen whisked Ashlyn away from the throne room, down the polished hallways. She deposited her in a plush bedroom, smiling warmly as Ashlyn settled into a chair. "I'll be right back," she promised, before sweeping from the room.

Ashlyn should have probably asked where she was going. She should have asked many questions in that moment. But she didn't voice a single one. She couldn't even bring herself to wonder privately about them, turning them over in her mind the way she would back home.

The queen had a stabilizing presence. With her gone, the room around Ashlyn turned strange and surreal. She stared at the wall, but didn't quite register it, her eyes somehow feeling unfocused in spite of the lack of blurring in her vision.

Perhaps that should have warranted some concern, but Ashlyn didn't feel concerned. Or much of anything. The inside of her mind held the same quality as the static on a television with no signal.

Time passed. Ashlyn was aware of it in the way that she was aware of the Earth spinning on its axis: vaguely, and only in theory. She stayed like that until a voice called at her from the doorway.

"Special girl! *Look* at what I've brought you."

The queen strode in, looking more solid and real than anything. She held in her arms a bundle of fabric, soft blues and whites.

Ashlyn blinked rapidly, her mind still slow and groggy. "It's a dress," she ventured.

"That's right!" The queen held it out, beaming. "Of course, there will be a grand party in your honor tonight. I'm sorry I couldn't get you more options on such short notice."

"It's alright." Ashlyn remembered Merrick's closet with a small pang, but pushed the feeling away. Clothes didn't matter. Azalea was the one who had insisted on her picking out her own clothing, and Azalea was a liar. Besides: "It's pretty."

It was. The light blue ball gown reached all the way to the floor, fitted at the bodice but with a large, bell-shaped skirt. A panel on the front spilled white lace over her skirt in a frothy wave. A white bow tied at the back of her waist completed the look.

"Oh, you look so lovely," the queen said. "What a fine princess you will be. Would you like help with your hair?"

"Sure." Ashlyn sat at a red vanity in the corner of the room. Her own reflection looked vague and dreamlike staring back at her, as though it belonged to someone else.

The queen settled behind her, hands deftly moving through the strands of Ashlyn's blonde hair. "It's funny, you know. My elder sister used to do this for *me*. It's strange to be on the other side of it."

"Is your sister here?" Ashlyn asked.

"No, no, this place would have no use for *her*." The queen sighed. "She had no sense for these things. Even her taste in reading was boring. No room for whimsy, that one."

This did, technically, answer Ashlyn's question. Just not the one she was *really* asking. "But is your sister . . . you know . . . like us?"

The queen eyed her kindly through the mirror. "Dead, you mean?"

Ashlyn swallowed. "Yes."

"I suppose she must be. My whole family, for that matter. It was so very long ago, although I wasn't there to see it."

This seemed to invite questions, but Ashlyn

couldn't bring herself to ask them. It would have been too nosy. Luckily, the queen didn't need prompting. She continued speaking, her fingers in Ashlyn's hair.

"I got sick. I was only a few years older than you, when it happened." The queen's voice was matter-of-fact. "Perhaps if I had been born in your time, there might have been help for it. But I wasn't, so I wasted away in bed. It was a drawn-out, ghastly affair."

"I'm sorry." Ashlyn's death had been quick, although it hadn't felt it at the time. Was that better or worse than a slow decline, watching death creep ever closer with its claws? "That sounds awful."

"It certainly wasn't pleasant," the queen agreed. "Remember how I told you that my sister used to do my hair? Well, she couldn't, toward the end. My hair was too thin and brittle to hold even a simple braid, and it kept falling out. It was . . ." She trailed off, frowning. Then she brightened. "Well! I suppose it doesn't matter, does it? It was so very long ago."

"I guess you're right," Ashlyn said, although she wasn't sure that was true. She didn't think she'd ever be able to approach her own death with such a casual tone.

The queen smiled, as if reading her thoughts. "Don't worry. It's different, when you're royalty. You'll find that things stop mattering so very much when you're able to get your way with the snap of a finger." She snapped her own fingers for emphasis. "Now, doesn't that sound nice?"

"It does." Although, if Ashlyn was being honest, she wasn't sure what she would ask for. The one thing she really wanted was for this to not be happening to her.

But if that was impossible, there were worse consolation prizes than a castle and a party in her honor.

The queen leaned over her shoulder, catching her gaze in the mirror. "You'll see. Everything will be just fine. Now, come along."

She offered a hand. Ashlyn took it, standing. Her new ballgown sat heavy on her shoulders, and she nearly overbalanced from the weight of it. How did the queen walk so lightly in her own dress, which was twice as grand?

The queen led her to a ballroom. The polished floor was the same dreamy red as the rest of the palace, but the walls were made of mirror glass. In them, the crowd of guests in their fine gowns and suits seemed three times as large. They all turned to face Ashlyn in unison, and her head spun slightly with the strangeness of it all.

"Where did they come from?" Ashlyn wondered.

"They're all for you, my dear," the queen replied in a warm whisper. Then, louder, she said to the crowd, "Bow to your new princess!"

One by one, the guests bowed. It stirred something in Ashlyn's chest to see them all so reverent. It wasn't a replacement for living, not really, but she wanted to cling to it, to dig her claws into it, to swallow the feeling whole. Maybe then, maybe if she played the queen's game, she'd stop feeling so hollow inside.

She breathed in. She breathed out. She smiled.

At some point, Ashlyn found herself dancing with a beautiful woman in a gray dress. She vaguely remembered the dance beginning, but she found that she couldn't remember who asked whom onto the polished floor.

"I'm Ashlyn," she ventured in a quiet voice. "What's your name?"

The woman blinked, her expression vague. "Would you like to . . . give me a name, your highness?"

"I . . . no." Ashlyn frowned. "I'd just like to know what your name *is*."

The woman stared at her, uncomprehending. Something slow and cold climbed up Ashlyn's spine, an emotion that it took her far too long to identify as dread.

"Something wrong, special girl?"

Ashlyn turned. The queen was looking at her inquisitively. Again, Ashlyn got the sense that she was solid, *real* in a way that the rest of them were not. She felt a sharpening in her own mind just to look at her.

The queen smiled. "Forgive me for cutting in," she said, slipping into place in front of Ashlyn. They began to dance.

"That woman . . ." Ashlyn began.

"Oh, that little doll?" The queen uttered a quiet laugh. "Don't fret over it, my dear. I certainly won't judge who you choose to play with."

Little doll. A shiver ran up her spine, although presently, Ashlyn couldn't remember why. "She didn't know her name," Ashlyn said. "I think she'd forgotten it."

"I suppose she might have," the queen replied. "Things have a way of getting lost in this place. But names aren't so important, are they? I haven't gone by mine for years now. I found it to be quite the burden."

Ashlyn didn't like this. But that dislike felt vague and difficult to hold, the dreamlike strains of the waltz threatening to wash it all away. They twirled, and Ashlyn willed herself to focus. "Will I forget?"

The queen cooed. "Never fear. I know that right now, things feel strange. But you aren't like the others. You'll get better control over it as time goes on. It just takes a bit of practice. But in no time, you'll be as certain as I am!"

Distantly, Ashlyn felt as though this statement should have bothered her. But as she twirled into the arms of another vague partner, she could no longer remember why.

Through The Doorway

shlyn stared at the canopy above her bed.

The ball had been fun. Or, at least, it had occupied her thoughts. But, eventually, it all became too overwhelming, and she could no longer stand the noise and the crowds. She'd gone back to her room and changed into pajamas, a blue button-down top with a white trim and a matching pair of pants.

Alone again, her thoughts began to turn dark and heavy. She couldn't sleep, but already she could feel that fugue state settling over her, the same one that had taken her over before the queen had burst into her room.

Was this to be her fate, then? Staring off into nothingness until summoned on a whim? Or would she, as the queen claimed, eventually gain control over this?

She wasn't sure. She wasn't sure if it *mattered*. Nothing felt like it mattered much anymore. Maybe drifting in this strange dream state would be kinder than clinging to the truth, anyway. She wouldn't be *herself*, but where had that ever gotten her?

A sudden warm weight landed on her chest, and Ashlyn gasped. But it wasn't a threat or some demon. It was only the black cat from before, staring down at her with its yellow gaze.

"Oh! It's you. Hello again, little friend." She reached up to scratch the cat behind its ears. It leaned into her touch, a low rumble starting up from deep within its chest. Ashlyn chuckled softly to herself. "You know, you're really not so strange. Are you sure you aren't just a normal cat?"

The cat grinned, revealing its unnervingly even human teeth.

"I see," Ashlyn replied. "That's fair."

The cat nuzzled into her hand for a while, twisting its face this way and that for her to scratch. Its purr seemed to echo through Ashlyn's ribs, making her feel solid and real in a way that even the presence of the queen didn't.

Finally, the cat leapt off her chest and plodded away on its little black feet. Ashlyn's heart gave a pang as it approached the cracked-open door, making as if to leave. But it didn't leave. Instead, it stood right at the threshold, a sliver of light illuminating its face as it turned and stared at her.

Ashlyn remained silent and still for what felt like minutes, but the cat didn't move or avert its gaze. "Little friend," she said. "Do you want me to follow you?"

Again, the cat smiled.

It seemed very strange to take orders from a cat, but Ashlyn supposed it was no stranger than becoming a princess just because a queen decided she was special. She stood, putting on her socks and sneakers with her pajamas. The palace floors were cold, after all.

The cat waited patiently through this, only striding out the door when Ashlyn walked toward it. She followed it down the hallways, nodding uncertainly at it when it turned around to stare at her.

After the noise and clatter of the ball, the silence in the hallways felt almost heavy. Ashlyn slowed her steps, not wanting to break that silence with the sound of her footsteps on marble. Even though she wasn't sure what she was hiding from. This wasn't like home, where walking around after curfew would get her scolded.

So why did she feel so uneasy?

The cat led her to the throne room. It seemed darker than it had before, in spite of the unchanging sky. As she stepped over the threshold, a woman shouted. Ashlyn jumped, clapping a hand over her mouth, but the shout wasn't aimed at her. It came, she realized, from behind the throne itself. The wall behind it was cracked open.

Right. The door. How had Ashlyn forgotten about the door? She crept forward, ears straining to catch the two familiar voices that echoed out.

"My queen—" Caul started.

"It's not *working*," the queen replied. Her voice was strange, an uncomfortable wet warble undermining the edges of her words. "Why isn't it working?"

There was a pause. Ashlyn could feel the tension in it, so thick that she swore that the air around her grew harder to breathe. "The snake grass *is* helping," Caul said, their voice measured and careful. "It's slowed the worst if it, and—"

"I don't want it slowed, I want it *stopped*!" The queen's voice took on a harsh, grating sound. "You were able to stop it before. What *happened*?"

"That was back when the licorice grove still existed," Caul replied. "It's—"

"Then make more!"

"I can't." Caul didn't raise their voice, even as the queen shouted. "Licorice hasn't grown here in decades. We've tried everything, your highness. I apologize."

The queen sighed. "I suppose it won't

matter soon. The girl will fix everything."

Ashlyn's pajamas were quite warm, made out of some sort of flannel, but that didn't stop the chill that ran up her spine. There was no question of who the queen was talking about. How many girls could she be referring to?

"Your highness," Caul said, sounding more cautious than ever. "I don't think you should be putting so much hope in her. You've tried this before—"

"—It's different now—"

"Alyssa, Ava, Abigail, Agatha. Countless others. They all ended the same—well, except for Azalea, but she was a unique case. And she was still a failure."

"But it's *different* now," the queen reiterated. "We figured out the problem. We have two of them. You agreed that would fix everything."

"I agreed with no such thing." Caul's tone was sharp, alarmed. "I offered a hypothesis. Nothing more."

The queen laughed. Even this was different from her usual laugh—not light bells but cracked, jagged metal. "You worry too much! You'll see. Everything will be just fine."

"I just want you to be careful," Caul replied. "You've already pushed yourself so hard doing this much. The glamours help, but they're not a cure."

"I *know* that." The queen's annoyance

sparked up a familiar memory: her mother, scolding her for something in that exact tone. "That's why I'm trying to *fix* it."

There was a long pause then. Ashlyn pressed herself up against the wall beside the gap, too frightened to actually peer through it. Her heart beat too fast in her chest, her breath thick in her throat.

"Do you ever think," Caul said slowly, "that maybe that's the problem? Trying to fix it, I mean."

"What are you talking about?" The queen's voice took on a warning note.

"It's just . . . the girl is young. She's already been dealt enough unfairness. This on top of it seems cruel."

"Fate is cruel." The queen sounded like she was sneering. "Just look at me. Do you think I deserve to look like this?"

"Of *course* not." Caul's answer came too fast, especially with how hesitant they sounded when they spoke next. "It's only . . . I hate to say it, but it's natural."

"There's nothing *natural* about this!"

"Please, Al—"

A flat sound echoed through the throne room, making Ashlyn wince. It took several seconds before she realized what it was: the sound of skin against skin. A slap.

"I am your queen," the queen hissed. "You will *not* address me by name."

They said that curiosity killed the cat, but the cat had vanished off to some secret feline place, and Ashlyn could no longer contain herself behind a veneer of caution and sense. She peered around the corner, through the crack.

The first thing she saw was Caul, on the floor and cowering with one hand covering their cheek, but Ashlyn barely spared them a glance. Most of her attention, and her dawning horror, went to the queen. Because she was no longer the queen Ashlyn knew.

A red dress clung to her skeletal form, hanging in rags. Her hair was long and stringy, and her fingernails were grown to near claws. But her skin, her skin was the worst—tinged blue and *sloughing* off, large patches gone to reveal bits of the bone.

This wasn't a woman at all. It was grotesque, a horror-movie parody of a rotting corpse.

Said corpse turned, fixing Ashlyn with a milky gaze. "Hello, special girl," she crooned.

Through The Window

Ashlyn cried out, stumbling back. The queen appeared in the doorway immediately, one skeletal hand reaching out.

"Don't run! Please. I can explain everything."

Ashlyn froze, more out of fear than obedience. The queen tutted, shaking her head. She pursed her lips in sympathy—although half of her face had rotted to teeth and bones, which rather mitigated any expected comfort. Behind her, a large portrait of the queen in her prime threw the difference between then and now into even sharper relief. "I know. It's a horrid sight, isn't it?" She sighed. "Caul, put the glamour back up."

"It seems like a waste at this point, I told

you—"

"Caul."

Caul winced, then waved a hand, mumbling a strange incantation. The air around the queen shimmered. Her ghastly features dissolved until she once again matched the portrait behind her—a portrait which had, strangely, begun to glow. The queen hummed. "That's better." She glanced behind her at the portrait as it dimmed. "Very useful, that. I had it done right when I . . . well, when it started. I knew it was important, for me not to forget. I needed to protect myself—body, heart, and soul. You understand, don't you?"

Ashlyn did not, in fact, understand. "What's going on? I heard you talking about me. Don't try to pretend you weren't."

"I would never lie to you, special girl." The queen reached out to touch Ashlyn's cheek, but didn't seem offended when Ashlyn jerked back. "I was hoping for more time to ease you into things, but . . . I suppose that's how it goes, isn't it?" She giggled, the sound as light as it had ever been. "It's just as well, though. You see, I'm afraid I find myself in a bit of a difficult spot."

"A . . . A bit," Ashlyn replied faintly. This seemed, to put it mildly, like *quite* the understatement.

But the queen only clapped her hands together, a cheerful smile lighting up her face. "*Only* a bit, I assure you. Because you're going to fix everything, special girl. Come, come. I have so much to tell you." She gestured to the open doorway, her eyes kind.

Ashlyn paused for a moment. Being in an enclosed space with the queen was the last thing she wanted to do, but she didn't feel like she had much of a choice. Where would she run? Was it even possible to run somewhere the queen wouldn't find her? She had her doubts.

She stepped inside. A circle of candles sat in the center of the room, and there was a long table pressed against one wall with a cauldron and what looked like plants scattered all across the surface. Against the opposite, dark red wall, a large window stood open to let in the cool dusk air, fluttering the debris of plants and paper on the floor.

"Excuse the mess," tittered the queen. "We were hardly expecting you so soon! And Caul keeps themself busy in here."

Ashlyn glanced to Caul. They hovered in the doorway, their hood pulled up to obscure their features. They didn't seem inclined to involve themself in the conversation, so she turned back to the queen instead. "What's happening?"

The queen hummed. "Ah, but it's so difficult to tell where to start . . . I suppose I'll have to start from the beginning!" She snapped her fingers. "Tell me, Ashlyn, do you know the name of this place?"

"Um . . ." Ashlyn tried to remember the names that Azalea had given her. "The Lost One's Forest? The Silent Wood?"

"Both perfectly serviceable names," the queen replied. "But it had a name before all of that, before everything. Back when I was alive, I called this place Wonderland."

"You . . . what?" Ashlyn struggled for a moment to gather her thoughts. "You mean, you came here before you died?"

"I more than came here, special girl! I invented it." The queen gave a little twirl, her expression wistful. "I invented it wholesale while I slept, and I filled it with the most marvelous of characters. The white rabbit . . . the mad hatter . . . the cheshire cat . . . and, of course, the queen of hearts." The queen winked. "All long gone now, of course."

Ashlyn suppressed a shiver at the queen's conspiratorial tone. "What happened to them?"

For the first time in this encounter, the queen's smile faded. "Well, after I died, Wonderland . . . changed. Dreams were never meant to be sustained, you know. But I couldn't bear to let this one fade away. I couldn't bear to let *myself* fade away. So I stayed. I usurped the queen, and I fortified her castle. It was my only choice. I couldn't let that night come for me. Don't you understand? It isn't *fair*."

It isn't fair. Hadn't Ashlyn said the same thing when she'd learned the truth? And, yet, the queen's words felt fundamentally wrong, wrong in a way that seemed to permeate every inch of the room. That feeling of unease grew as the queen continued to speak.

"But even so, my lovely cast of characters vanished. The dormouse disappeared. The mad hatter babbled himself into oblivion, leaving only his top hat behind. Even the *caterpillar* left." For a moment the queen looked truly wretched, but her expression quickly smoothed into calm. "But I realized I didn't have to be alone. I was able to find . . . new friends. People who passed, but didn't quite pass *on*." The queen smiled. "Caul arrived first. But others soon followed. I made them knights, servants, handmaidens. It was a joyous time."

Again, Ashlyn looked to Caul. The way that they turned away seemed almost purposeful, as though they were trying to conceal their expression from Ashlyn. Or from the queen. Maybe they were afraid that she'd read something less than "joyous" on their face.

"But things started to change again," the queen continued. "My court . . . they didn't appreciate what they had. They wanted to go on." Her face twisted, caught in a horrid dance between rage and grief. "They were going to let Wonderland *rot*! They *wanted* my dream to wither!"

Ashlyn flinched back at the intensity in her voice, half expecting a blow. But it never came.

The queen took a breath as if to steady herself, pressing her palms together.

"I was able to handle it," she said. "I *have* been handling it. But there have been . . . side-effects. Wonderland falling to ruin, and my body . . . Well. You saw, didn't you?"

Now, at last, it seemed as though the queen was looking for a response. Ashlyn wrapped her arms around herself. "I still don't understand. What does this have to do with me?"

The queen smiled. "Because some souls . . . some souls that come here are special. I began to realize a pattern. When souls came through not realizing they had died . . . they shared some similarities." She began to tick off traits on her fingers. "All young. All girls. All with names that began with the letter A. I realized that they, too, could hold power over this place. They could shape it in the way I could. They could help."

Ashlyn frowned. "What did you do to them? Why was Azalea so afraid of you?"

"I'll admit, my methods were . . . unorthodox at first. You mustn't blame me." The queen actually laughed. "My knights heal up quick, and they can't die. I had no reason to believe that my special girls wouldn't be the same way! Although I learned after the first few."

A chill settled in Ashlyn's stomach. "You killed them?"

"They were already dead! They just . . . didn't heal. More like the inhabitants of Wonderland than the knights." The queen locked eyes with Ashlyn. "It's not *just* whimsy, or cruelty. You have to understand, blood has been useful thus far. Spilling the original queen's blood was how I got my power. Blood from the knights keeps our castle fortified and strong. And special blood . . ." She smiled. "Oh, don't look at me like that! I won't hurt you."

"Then what will you do?" Ashlyn had half a mind to run to the window. But her curiosity was too strong. "What do you want with me?"

"Being a queen is useful, in many ways. But it has some limitations." The queen frowned, oddly thoughtful. "It's difficult for me to explain how I know these things. Wonderland and I are one and the same, so I can't be the one to fix it. I need help. A princess. And that's why all my attempts have failed. I can't shed blood to end this. But you, my special girl . . . You can do it."

Ashlyn trembled. "You want me to . . . You really want me to . . ."

Unbothered by the horror in Ashlyn's voice, the queen clapped her hands. "Alright! You can bring her in."

A pair of knights stomped in, dragging a smaller figure between them. Bound in shackles, she stumbled to keep up with their strides, trembling as though exhausted. Her long brown hair hung in her face, but Ashlyn had no trouble recognizing her.

"Azalea!"

"You won't have any problems with this one," the queen said. "Don't worry. She isn't the type to fight back. Far too weak-willed."

And, as though it were the most natural thing in the world, the queen slipped a knife into Ashlyn's hand.

Ashlyn stared at the blade, unable to make sense of the object in the context of her sudden possession of it. Surely, the queen couldn't be asking her to . . . couldn't think that she would *ever* . . .

"I know it's difficult to ask of you, but it will be quick," the queen promised. "The vorpal blade's enchanted, stronger than any ax. You can have it done in one swipe. And then Wonderland will be restored. *I* will be restored. We can spend eternity in the most beautiful dream. That's worth a little sacrifice, isn't it?"

Ashlyn stared at Azalea. Azalea stared back. Her green eyes were wide and horrified—as if, in that moment, she were staring not at Ashlyn, but at the queen. Azalea thought that Ashlyn was going to do it, she realized. Azalea thought that Ashlyn was going to sacrifice her at the altar of this twisted dream.

And what reason did she have to doubt it? The last thing Ashlyn did to her was send her to the dungeon. The last thing she'd proclaimed was that she didn't care if she became cruel. Nothing she had done, she realized, would have given Azalea any reason to believe that she would show mercy in this moment.

Ashlyn had made her choice. She'd aligned herself with the queen.

And it hadn't fixed anything.

Ashlyn brought the knife down. The queen was right, something had enchanted the blade. It cut through Azalea's chains as though they were nothing more than tissue paper, severing her from the guard's grasp.

"What—" Azalea started, but Ashlyn was already hauling her to her feet, shoving her toward the open window.

"Run!"

The queen let out a cheated, angry shout. But Ashlyn still had the blade in her hand, and when the queen lurched toward them, she lashed out, slashing her across her face. The queen screeched, holding her face as the glamour flickered, revealing the rotting corpse once more.

"My face. My *face*!"

Ashlyn turned from her and flung herself out the window, dragging Azalea with her. They both hit the ground hard, Ashlyn's soft pajamas ripping at the knee. She found she didn't care much. She offered a hand to Azalea, breathing heavy. "Let's go. I'll . . . I'll protect us, okay?"

Azalea stared at her hand for a long

moment. As though she were considering slapping it away, fleeing, or simply laying down in the dirt and ignoring the offering entirely. Ashlyn wasn't sure that she would blame her for any of those things.

Instead, she took it, and let Ashlyn pull her to her feet.

- *18* -

Through The Cottage

The journey out through the hedges seemed too slow, as though they were twisting around and back, keeping them trapped. Even though she could still hear the queen shrieking from the castle behind them, Ashlyn still felt sure that she would be waiting for them around every turn with her rotting face and skeletal form. When did directions ever make sense here?

At least when they had arrived at the castle, she'd been able to find some comfort in Azalea's presence beside her. But she did not feel that comfort now. Azalea was still with her, true, but she was different now, hollow-eyed and silent. No longer a companion. No longer a friend.

Finally, the hedges came to an end. Ashlyn

let out a sigh as the familiar forest engulfed them. "Where should we go now?"

Azalea didn't react to her freedom. She only stared ahead, her voice dull. "I don't know."

Ashlyn regarded her for a moment. Should she say something? An apology, at least? Only simple words of regret seemed to not be enough to erase what she had done. She doubted it would be enough to remove the haunted look from the other girl's eyes.

She gripped her blade a little tighter. "Well, let's try to put some distance between us and the castle, anyway. We need to keep moving."

Azalea laughed. It was, Ashlyn thought, her most pitiful attempt at the sound yet. "We *do*, don't we?"

The question didn't feel as rhetorical as it sounded, but Ashlyn didn't know how to respond to it. Instead, she started walking. After a few moments, Azalea dragged herself in line beside her.

Ashlyn wasn't sure how long they walked. The castle was difficult to avoid, always looming, but Ashlyn kept it to her peripheral vision, and slowly it began to fade into the distance. A trick of the forest, or evidence of Ashlyn's supposed power within this place? She wasn't sure, but the queen's shrieks faded until the sounds of the forest swallowed them, and that felt far more important than wondering how.

And, then, they came upon a familiar round door. Relief coursed through Ashlyn's veins as she rushed to it, pounding on it with the hand not clutching the blade. "Hello? Hello, *please*, is anyone home?"

The door creaked open. Lucy stood there, warmth emanating from behind her. "What is— oh, goodness, what *happened* to you two?"

Ashlyn wasn't sure what tipped Lucy off to the fact that something was wrong—Azalea's worn out state and hollow eyes or Ashlyn's blood-stained pajamas and white-knuckled grip on her blade. Either way, Ashlyn found herself utterly unable to give a response. "I—I . . ." Horrifyingly, a lump began to form in her throat, her eyes stinging with tears.

"*Oh.*" All at once, Lucy's arms enveloped her. Which was nice, because Ashlyn couldn't recall the last time she had been more in need of a hug. "Oh, dear, you two come in now. You'll be alright."

Ashlyn allowed Lucy to lead her inside, doing her best to pull herself together. Breaking down and sobbing sounded appealing in its way, but also decidedly unhelpful. She needed to hunker down and figure out what to do next, she needed to . . . she needed to . . .

Only there *was* no next. Ashlyn was dead; her days of 'nexts' were behind her. This forest had her trapped instead—not even in her own dream, but in the dream of some desperate queen.

A weight settled on her chest. She began to wonder if it wasn't just her own betrayal that had put that hollow look in Azalea's eyes. After all, she knew the truth, too.

As if summoned by this realization, Azalea spoke. "May I use your bedroom again? I'm . . . very tired. I'd like to rest."

"Of course," Lucy replied. "Whatever you need."

Azalea started toward the bedroom. Quite without thinking, Ashlyn reached out and grabbed her wrist. Azalea startled a little at the contact, then looked up, her green eyes oddly flat. It made Ashlyn's chest ache, but more than that, it made her scared. It was too easy to imagine her expression having been much the same, when she fell into that enchanted slumber Ashlyn had roused her from.

"Azalea," she asked. "Are you . . . going to be okay?"

Azalea closed her eyes for a long moment. When she opened them, some life had come back into them—not light, but at least that haunted hollow look had receded somewhat. "I will be," she replied. "I just need to rest for a little while. It won't be like . . . like before."

"Okay." Ashlyn was glad that Azalea had understood her question, however vaguely worded. As strange as things were between them now, she didn't want Azalea to end up in another tree. "Okay, that's fine."

Azalea vanished into the bedroom, and Lucy gently led Ashlyn into the living room. Kazuo sat in the window, staring moodily out of it. Merrick appeared to be reading a book, but upon closer inspection, he was holding it upside down. It didn't matter much in the long run, anyway—when he saw Ashlyn, he flung the tome thoughtlessly to the side.

"Well, hello there! How fares your adventure?"

"Terrible," Ashlyn replied. "Terrible, it's . . . it's all gone wrong. Even after everything I tried, everything I've done . . . none of it matters. I won't ever be able to go home."

She slumped down onto the couch, burying her face in her hands. Lucy sat beside her, putting a warm hand on her back. "I understand. It's a difficult thing to come to terms with."

"You don't understand," Ashlyn snapped. "We can't go home because we're dead, don't you get it? We *died*."

Ashlyn regretted the words as soon as she'd said them. But the others didn't react how she had when confronted with this information. Kazuo didn't even stir from his place by the window; Merrick's expression only softened slightly, and when Lucy put a hand to her mouth, it was more thoughtful than horrified.

"That's right," she murmured. "Of course."

"I suppose that *is* a wrong turn, in its own

way," Merrick mused.

"I've been saying it all along," Kazuo muttered. "We haven't got any time left, no time at all."

"You all *knew*?" Ashlyn's voice shot up an octave. "Why didn't you say something earlier?"

"It's more complicated than that," A deep furrow had appeared between Lucky's brows, as though she were concentrating very hard. "It isn't so much that we forgot, it's just . . . holding onto that information in a way that's tangible, is . . . oh, I don't know how to describe it."

"It's like remembering that the sky is blue when you're trapped underground," Merrick offered.

"It's really not much like that at all, but thank you for trying, Merrick."

"I think I understand what you're saying, though," Ashlyn ventured. "It might have something to do with the queen, she . . . before, people wanted to stop her from keeping them here, so she must have done something to confuse you."

That wouldn't have applied to Azalea, though. Ashlyn's chest ached, but after everything, she wasn't really sure she had the right to feel upset about Azalea keeping the information from her.

"You met the queen?" Lucy asked.

"She . . . She took me in. She said I was

special, said that this place . . . that *Wonderland* was going to fall apart, but that I could keep it going forever." Ashlyn held out the knife. "She gave me this—called it the Vorpal blade—and wanted me to . . . to . . ." She shook her head. "I couldn't do it. I couldn't do what she asked me to. It was too awful."

"Oh, dear." Lucy wrapped an arm around her. "It's alright."

"I just don't know what to do *now*," Ashlyn nearly wailed. "I spent all that time, and did . . . I did some stuff I'm not proud of. And for what? To sit and wait for this place to unravel?"

"Would that really be so terrible?"

Ashlyn looked up then. Lucy was looking at her kindly, but not without a certain degree of sadness. It was the look one wore at the bedside of a terminal patient.

"All of this time, you've been so sure that you needed to get home," she said gently. "And maybe you were right all along. Because letting this place fade, moving on . . . that *is* going home, isn't it? Just . . . in a bit of a different way than you had thought."

Ashlyn looked down at the blade in her hands. It was true, she was unwilling and unable to do what the queen asked of her to sustain this place. But, still . . .

"It's not fair." Tears slipped down Ashlyn's cheeks, unbidden. "It's not *fair*."

Merrick sat on her other side. His usually

mischievous expression had dimmed, replaced by a smile so sympathetic that made her want to weep harder. He put a hand on her shoulder.

"You're right," he murmured. "It isn't fair."

It was, perhaps, the last thing she expected to hear from Merrick, if only because it sounded so *sincere*. She looked up at him, searching his expression for some sort of tease. But there was only that quiet sympathy.

"It's funny," he said, near conversational. "I always considered myself to be rather extraordinary. Prided myself on it. Ironic, then, that my end turned out to be so tragically mundane. An old car, bad brakes, and then . . ." He made a vague, theatrical gesture, flicking his fingers into space. "How many, do you think, ended in just that way? As young as me, or even younger? As young as *you*?"

Ashlyn could feel him working up to a point, in his own way. She sniffled, wiping at her eyes. "What are you saying?"

"I'm saying, it's a horrible feeling. But you aren't alone in that feeling—not here in this place, and not back in the world we left. And perhaps that's part of what makes it so terrible. But isn't there comfort in that, too? Curious, how those two things can both be true at once." And then, of all things, he winked. "But maybe, in truth, it isn't so curious at all."

19

Through The . . .

Ashlyn sat outside, staring at the trees.

She hadn't gone far—still in the yard of Merrick's home, sitting in the brittle brown grass. But she couldn't stand feeling so cooped up in there any longer. She wanted to spend as much time as possible outside, until . . . well, *until*.

Ashlyn shivered, pulling her newly borrowed jacket around herself. She hadn't had Azalea to help her pick out an outfit this time, but she'd managed anyway: black jeans, a sweater patterned with stars, and fingerless gloves made of black lace that were even more impractical than the first. A choice she made all on her own, too late to do her any good.

She wasn't quite sure why she'd bothered.

She didn't even really know why she was waiting here. Or maybe she did, but she couldn't bring herself to think about it. Lucy made it sound like letting this place fade away was the best option, but Ashlyn wasn't sure she could agree. She didn't want to be *dead*.

But . . . she was already dead. And even lingering here in this dream was not a proper substitute for being alive. Not in a way that mattered.

Her chest ached. But even as she grieved herself, she had to admit that Merrick, too, had a point. She was hardly the first person in this world to die young, or in unfair circumstances. For that matter, none of the people here looked old enough to have died of natural causes: Kazuo was only just starting to go gray; both Lucy and Merrick were young adults. And Azalea was Ashlyn's age.

As if summoned by her thoughts, Azalea appeared in the doorway. She now wore sturdy brown slacks and a cream-colored blouse with a dark blue bodice that laced up the front. And her eyes had changed, too. She still looked tired, but the haunted energy that had clung to her before had receded somewhat, or at least lost the rawest of its edges.

She sat beside Ashlyn in the grass, her gaze set on the horizon. Ashlyn looked out as well, feeling the silence thick and heavy between them. Eventually, it grew too much for her to bear. "I'm sorry," she blurted, before she could think herself out of it. "I'm so, so sorry I got angry at you."

Azalea sighed, her shoulders slumping. "You're allowed to be angry," she said. "I'm sorry, too. I shouldn't have lied to you."

"Being angry doesn't justify what I *did*, though." Ashlyn leaned forward, palms pressed in the brittle grass. "You didn't deserve that. I really don't know what came over me. I know it's not an excuse, but it's the truth."

Azalea nodded. Finally, mercifully, she looked in Ashlyn's direction. "I can imagine. I wasn't . . . I wasn't like you, when I found out. But it *did* break me. I didn't want that for you. *Couldn't* do that to you. Not when you were so . . . so hopeful." She sighed, shaking her head. "But what I did wasn't kindness, even if I told myself it was. It was selfishness. Being around you, I almost remembered how it was to feel . . ."

"To feel what?" Ashlyn prompted.

"*Anything*," Azalea whispered. "I didn't think I had it in me anymore. But then you came. And I thought . . ." Her voice broke off with an odd noise. "Well. It doesn't matter now."

The weight in her voice frightened Ashlyn more than anything the queen had done. "Learning the truth really made you feel that empty?"

Azalea made her most pathetic attempt at a

laugh yet. "Worse than empty. Hopeless. I just wanted to stop." She glanced over at Ashlyn, her expression oddly vulnerable. "But I was like that even before I died. It's *why* I died."

"Oh." Ashlyn lifted a hand to her mouth. "You mean . . ."

"I do." Azalea looked down again, long hair covering her face. "Is it any wonder that I chose sleep in this world? Even before, I was always so *tired*. All the time. Even the things that once brought me joy only made me feel hollow inside. And what did it matter? I didn't have the energy to mourn it. I didn't have the energy to care. Everything, everything took effort. So eventually I decided I . . . didn't want to put in the effort anymore." Her voice broke, and she reached one hand beneath the curtain of her hair to wipe at her face. "The queen knew. You heard the way she talked about me, didn't you? Weak. Aimless. Maybe she's right. Maybe that's why I clung to you so hard."

Ashlyn remembered the words. They'd seemed cruel at the time, but now they seemed doubly so, and unfair in the bargain. Like when her parents scolded her for the bouts of anxiety she couldn't control. She cleared her throat. "But you woke up. When I called for you in the forest, and then again in Merrick's house. You woke up."

Azalea looked at her. Her pale cheeks were slightly blotchy, but her green eyes were clear.

"You sounded like you needed help."

Ashlyn was quiet for a long moment. There were plenty of things to say in this moment, and many of them felt like the wrong thing. But the worst thing, she thought, would have been to say nothing.

So very carefully, she said, "I think that might be the strongest thing anyone's ever done."

Azalea's face broke then, and in spite of everything, Ashlyn found it easy to close the distance between them. She wrapped her arms around Azalea's shoulders, and Azalea clung to her shirt, and together they sat as the forest rustled and Azalea heaved in one tortured breath, then another.

"I wish I'd stayed," Azalea whispered. "Just a little longer. I wish I would have stayed to see the stars more."

"Yeah." Ashlyn's voice broke. "Yeah, me too."

They pulled apart after some indeterminate amount of time, but the chilly distance between them did not return. Azalea kept her hand over Ashlyn's, their fingers tangled together—not careless, but casual, as though they were meant to be like that.

"So, what should we do now?" Azalea asked.

That was the question. Ashlyn frowned at the horizon, searching for any signs of decay.

She couldn't see them, but the weight in her chest told her they were coming. "This place is fading," she murmured quietly. "And . . . Lucy seems to think we should let it."

"You can't do that," a voice replied.

Ashlyn startled. Caul stood at the edge of the trees, hood down. They seemed even paler than usual, dark circles prominent under their eyes. Despite their pitiful expression, Ashlyn tensed, putting an arm in front of Azalea as if to shield her.

Caul raised their hands, palms out as if in supplication. "Don't worry. I've come alone."

Perhaps hearing the commotion, Merrick poked a head out the window, his top hat just barely fitting through. "Caul! Have you finally considered taking me up on my offer?"

"No. Yes. I don't know." Caul ran both hands through their lank hair, fingers hooked like claws.

Ashlyn's original, startled burst of emotion had since faded, but in its wake remained a sort of low, droning dread that she saw mirrored in Azalea's face when she turned to look. "What did you mean, about us not being able to let Wonderland fade?"

Lucy, who had appeared in the doorway, leaned against the wall, arms folded over her chest and face uncharacteristically stern. "Yes, I'm a bit curious about that as well."

"You don't understand how it's gotten."

Caul's voice dipped low, urgent. "The queen . . . she's always been ruthless, but it's different now. If we let Wonderland die, she'll destroy all of us in the process, just because she can."

Silence settled over them like a thick coat of snow over a field, growing heavier and colder by the moment. When Ashlyn finally broke it, her voice shook. "What are you suggesting? Because I won't do what she wanted me to do." She squeezed Azalea's hand, gratified when Azalea squeezed back. "I couldn't. I wouldn't, ever."

"I'm not suggesting that," Caul snapped. "But the queen *has* to be dealt with." They took a shaky breath, their skin looking nearly gray. "She needs to be . . . taken care of."

Ashlyn blanched. "You mean we have to *kill* her?"

"Insomuch as anyone can kill anyone here," Merrick mused, earning him a glare from Lucy.

"We wouldn't be able to land a hit on her," she said in the sharp voice of someone who had, perhaps, tried on more than one occasion to do just that.

"*We* wouldn't. But *they* can." Caul pointed, unmistakably, at Ashlyn and Azalea.

"What do you mean?" Azalea asked. Her voice was very quiet.

"The queen was right about one thing: you both have a connection to this place, and its power. And you have the vorpal blade. Driving it through the queen's heart is the only way to end all of this safely."

Ashlyn's stomach churned. "You mean . . . we have to . . ."

"I'll do it."

Ashlyn turned. Azalea stood, her usually dreamy face focused, her voice quiet but determined.

"The queen has gone unchecked for too long," Azalea said. "A cruel puppeteer, with us as her unwilling puppets. I can't allow myself to stand for it. Not anymore."

Ashlyn stepped up beside Azalea, examining the other girl's expression. "Are you sure?"

Azalea's expression shifted, a minute change held mostly in the corners of her eyes and the tightness of her lips. "Would you believe me if I told you there was a time that I would have welcomed the queen's wrath? A total destruction of self, down to the soul. But I don't think I want that anymore. Being with you, I remembered how to hope." She squared her shoulders. "And I want to hope that, beyond this dream, there's something better."

Ashlyn's eyes stung with unshed tears, both at the conviction in Azalea's voice and the content of her words. "I'll go with you," she said. "We'll do it together."

She wasn't sure if she could express why

she wanted to go. Only that Azalea's statement had settled into her chest, resonating in her heart along with Lucy's acceptance, Merrick's understanding, and Kazuo's diligence. As much as she still ached, that had to mean something.

Luckily, Azalea seemed to understand. Her gaze softened. "Okay," she said. "Together."

20

Through.

The palace was falling apart.

Great sections of the red castle crumbled to ruin, all jagged edges and gaping chasms where towers had once been. The hedges were dull and lifeless, barren branches that looked as though they'd snap into dust at the slightest provocation.

"It really *is* ending." Lucy stared at the castle with the oddest sort of expression, brows tilted and furrows around her eyes. Considering what Ashlyn knew of her time in it, she couldn't begrudge the note of satisfaction she saw in them.

"And we'll end with it, if we don't do *something*." In contrast, Caul looked distinctly uncomfortable, as though prepared to bolt at any moment. "Are we going to go through with this, or are we going to just stand here?"

Ashlyn looked to Azalea. She stared at the crumbling castle, her expression harder to read than Lucy's. But she gripped the vorpal blade tight enough to turn her knuckles white, her hand shaking just slightly with the effort of it.

Ashlyn couldn't blame her. She felt more than a little shaky herself. Felt, in fact, a little like she was about to vibrate out of her skin with the fear and anticipation of it all.

Azalea's voice was steady, though. That helped.

"I'm ready. Let's go."

Ashlyn glanced over her shoulder. Merrick and Kazuo stood at the tree line, along with the members of their group that had played chess with them earlier. They would wait there while she and Azalea entered with Lucy and Caul. Merrick caught Ashlyn's eye and tipped her a wink.

Walking through the hedges went much faster this time. Several large sections had withered and died, leaving them walking across a flat plain of dying earth, dust kicking up around their shoes.

In no time, they'd reached the steps of the palace. These were in similar disrepair, and a suit of armor sat where a hyperventilating knight once did. Ashlyn could tell by the awkward slump of the metal that no one was inside the suit now, however. A sword lay sprawled in the dirt.

"I hope they're alright," Azalea said, looking down at the suit of armor with a frown.

"Maybe they just fled," offered Lucy. "The armor *is* very heavy, more than armor has any right to be. The queen had it made for aesthetics and barbarism, not practicality."

Ashlyn hoped, for the suit's former owner's sake, that Lucy was right. Because the images that the armor conjured in her mind—images of a body collapsing in on itself, turning to dust until even its soul was no more—made her pulse race in painful, rabbit-footed beats. Had it already begun? Was the fall of Wonderland already affecting those trapped in its web? Just how much time did they have left?

Even with her own hesitance, the thought made her feel cold.

A low growl broke Ashlyn from her thoughts, echoing through the ruined hedges. Another growl echoed it, and another, and another, until there was a whole chorus of growls and snarls and harsh, angry barks. The queen's wolves slinked out of the branches. They seemed emaciated, their fur matted, but their teeth were sharp as ever, their eyes full of feral rage.

Lucy scooped up the sword from the ground just in time to slash at the first wolf as it leapt. "Run! Get inside and finish this, we'll hold them off." Beside her, Caul blasted another wolf with a bolt of green magic from their wide sleeve.

Ashlyn grabbed Azalea by the sleeve, dragging her inside. "Come on!"

"But Lucy and Caul—"

"You heard Lucy. The best way to help them is by finding the queen!"

The doors thudded shut behind them, muffling the clash of Lucy's sword, the buzz of Caul's powers, and the howls of the wolves. In their wake, the silence of the castle seemed ominously thick. Ashlyn couldn't help the guilt that settled in her chest. Azalea had obviously wanted to help, the way she had wanted to help the guards before, but . . .

"I'm sorry," she said.

"You're right, though." Azalea swiped at her eyes with a sleeve, more a gesture of exhaustion than any attempt to dispel tears. "You're right. We need to end this before it's too late."

Their footsteps echoed through the ruined castle. A floor tile caught beneath Ashlyn's sneaker, skittering with a glass-like tinkle ahead of them. From ahead, as if in response, a low groan echoed from the entrance of the throne room.

A shiver ran up Ashlyn's spine. "That's her," she whispered. Because even now, she recognized the voice of the queen.

The throne room was empty. But the door

behind the throne was ajar, and it was from there that the groan issued. Ashlyn exchanged a terse glance with Azalea, who nodded once. Together, they crept forward, peering through the door.

The queen's portrait still hung on the wall, as pristine as ever. Beneath it, the real queen was as far from pristine as she could get. Hunched over like an animal, her stringy hair hung in her face, her once magnificent dress now tattered rags. The keening that issued from her lips was near feral, every bit as awful as her wolves.

Still, some of her strange brand of cunning remained, because she sensed Ashlyn and Azalea the moment they stepped up to the doorway. Her rotting face jerked up as though yanked by invisible strings, her eyes dull with anger.

"*You*," she snarled. "All of this . . . this *rot* . . . is because of *you*."

Ashlyn froze. She thought she understood the horror of what the queen was—of what she had become. But seeing it all over again was horrifying. It seemed more clear than ever that she was looking at someone who should not still exist—who *could* not exist in the world that was sane and good. Maybe she hadn't "made her peace" with her fate in the same way that others had, but even she couldn't deny the base facts.

Death was unfair. *This* was worse.

"*You*!" The queen snarled again, guttural,

terrible. She leapt.

Ashlyn had no time to flee, to flinch, even to scream. But Azalea, somehow, did. And what Azalea did with that time was throw herself in between the queen and Ashlyn, the vorpal blade held aloft.

The queen impaled herself on it, the blade burying itself in her chest to the hilt.

She stumbled forward, knocking into Ashlyn and Azalea as she did. Both scattered out of her way, so that their positions switched around—the queen now hovering in the entrance to the odd back room, and Azalea and Ashlyn inside of it. The queen stood there, swaying back and forth, as though at any moment she would collapse into a pile of old bones and rot.

But the queen did not collapse. Instead, she began to laugh. The dagger in her chest wobbled with the force of it, but no blood spread to surround the wound. It was as if Azalea had stabbed some inanimate object—a wooden puppet, perhaps, or else a doll made of foam.

"You really thought *that* would defeat me?" the queen hissed.

"Oh, no," Azalea whispered, "Ashlyn, *look*."

It took Ashlyn a moment to understand what Azalea was referring to—*everything* about this was so terrible; what specifically had put that note in Azalea's voice? But then she saw. The window they'd escaped out before had collapsed into rubble, leaving no gap outside. And with the queen blocking the only other exit, there was no escape from this room.

There was no escape, and the queen still wasn't gone.

"I'll show you," she growled. "I might not be able to save Wonderland, but I'll still make you suffer."

She leapt at Azalea with an animalistic cry.

Azalea cried out as she hit the wall, shoving the queen back with as much force as she could muster. Ashlyn threw herself on the queen's back, wrapping her hands around the hilt of the blade and yanking up. It tore through the queen's chest, but then she reared back, and Ashlyn went flying, the knife clattering to the ground.

"That won't work!" The queen snarled, turning on her with feral anger. There was a gaping hole in her chest, lined by a jagged row of ribs that had snapped like twigs under the force of the vorpal blade.

It didn't make sense. Azalea had stabbed her right where her heart should have been. Had Caul lied?

Or was her heart not in her chest at all?

Ashlyn didn't turn to face the portrait, but she knew it was there. And she remembered what the queen had said. *I needed to protect myself—body, heart, and soul.*

"Azalea," Ashlyn cried out, "Give me the blade!"

There was a moment of fear, then—fear that Azalea wouldn't trust her after everything, even if she had forgiven her. But Azalea didn't hesitate. She scooped up the knife and threw it to Ashlyn.

And Ashlyn caught it.

There was no time to think. No time to dwell on the implications, to fear the results. Any moment the queen would be upon her. Ashlyn whirled, and with every ounce of strength she had, she drove the vorpal blade into the queen's portrait.

Behind her, the queen *screamed*.

The scream was awful, not because it was feral, but because it was *human*. When Ashlyn turned, the queen was wailing, her legs collapsing beneath the weight of her own body, bent at unnatural angles.

"*No!*" She clawed at her face, leaving deep, bloodless furrows. "No, it's not fair, it's not fair, it's not *fair*!"

In spite of everything, Ashlyn felt a pang—not quite of remorse, but of pity. As she watched, the queen crumpled to nothing but old bones, and soon, not even that. She fell to ash, dissolved into the floorboards. The queen was gone.

For a long moment, all of Wonderland seemed to hold its breath.

And then, it began. Wonderland did not crumple to ash as the queen had. The castle faded, melting into the hedges, the trees. Familiar faces swam out at her: Lucy, awestruck; Caul, painfully hopeful. Merrick clapped his hands together joyfully, and Kazuo let out a sigh that sounded a lot like relief. Ashlyn had the most curious sensation of being inside of a book as the pages fluttered shut—she swore she could almost smell the parchment, warm and comforting.

And in the gaps between those "pages," a darkness spread. But this was not the darkness of the well. It was not cold, and it was not empty. It was a swirling mass of the richest dark blue and purple, speckled with bright silver.

"Oh, Ashlyn," Azalea breathed, her eyes shining. "Look at the *stars*."

Ashlyn went to her, taking her hand. Wonderland continued to fold in on itself, gentle as silk. Merrick laughed and grabbed Caul by the hands, waltzing them into the dark. Lucy, already half-embraced by the dark, gave the girls one warm smile before fading away. Kazuo shook his head, a rueful grin on his face. "Finally," he murmured. "Enough wasting time."

One by one, people vanished into the night. But one familiar figure was not walking away. It walked toward Ashlyn instead, weaving between trees and sheets of glass and checkerboards on sweet black paws. Only, Ashlyn now realized, it wasn't black at all. It was the same rich velvet color of the night, its fur speckled with stars.

Warmth filled her chest as Ashlyn knelt down to greet the cat. "Hello, little friend."

Azalea knelt, too, her gaze fixed on the cat. She held out a hand that trembled slightly, and when she spoke, it was almost too quiet to hear. "Am I . . . Will it be okay for me, too?"

The cat sniffed her hand. Then, it craned its neck, gently head-butting her palm as it purred. Azalea let out a wet laugh, rubbing it behind the ears.

Then, she turned to Ashlyn. "Are you ready?"

Ashlyn pondered this question for a moment. It wasn't fear that kept her from answering right away, or regret or anger. Those emotions, like Wonderland, were folding in on themselves, indexed in the pages of a story that was now rapidly approaching its end. But, still, there was one thing she wanted to do.

She closed the distance between them, kissing Azalea sweetly on the lips. Azalea kissed her back.

"Now I am," she said when she finally pulled away.

Azalea smiled. She took Ashlyn's hand as they got to their feet. And, together, they walked into the night.

21

Epilogue

nd that is how the story ends. Not with "and they all lived happily ever after," as that would not be true. Not even with "the end," which would be just as dishonest.

It often takes my young listeners time to digest. They ask all the questions you could expect one to ask in that situation: What happened to Ashlyn and Azalea next? Did they vanish, or find themselves in a new place? Were they together? Were they happy?

I answer all these questions the same: is there any answer I could give that would satisfy you?

Some make up their own endings. Some only nod solemnly, and try to understand.

And perhaps, one day, I tell this tale to a pair

of young girls who find their way giggling into my library. Perhaps, at the end of it, the blonde girl thanks me and remarks on the evenness of my smile. Perhaps the green-eyed girl hands me a flower and reminds me to look at the stars tonight—it's supposed to be a clear one, and wouldn't it be a shame to miss something so lovely?

Perhaps I watch them through the window as they leave. Perhaps the library's resident cat will join me, staring out at the girls with an interest that seems almost knowing. His eyes may even reflect the light in a way that seems to turn them silver, like the very stars that girl advised me to admire.

But he won't smile. He's only a cat, after all.

More by Jillian Maria

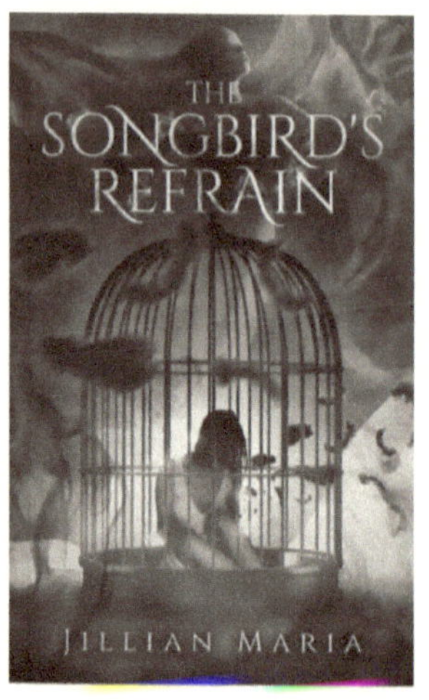

Elizabeth is rarely noticed—until she's noticed in the worst way, by an evil witch who kidnaps and curses her. Will she find the strength to break free? Can she find the courage to even try?

City girl Lydia is expecting a boring week in her grandmother's small town of Fairbrooke. But that changes when she meets Eden, a curious girl hunting fae treasure in the forest.

 **Jillian Maria** enjoys tea, pretty dresses, and ripping out pieces of herself to put in her novels. She writes the books she wants to read, prominently featuring women who are like her in some way or another. A great lover of horror, thriller and mystery novels, most of her stories have some of her own fears lurking in the margins. When she isn't willing imaginary people into existence, she's pursuing a career in public relations and content marketing. A Michigan native, Jillian spends what little free time she has hanging out with her friends, reading too much, singing along to musical numbers, and doting on her cat.